COWBOY KARMA

MIA HOPKINS

Ebook ISBN 978-0-9979922-0-5

Print ISBN 978-0-9979922-1-2

Originally published in 2016 by Little Stone Press

Second edition: October 2025

Cover by Bloom with Brynn

Cowboy Karma is a work of fiction. Names, places, and incidents either are products of the author's imagination or are used fictitiously. Any resemblance to actual events, locales, or persons, living or dead, is entirely coincidental.

To Crissy, the sweetest, most creative girl/unicorn I've ever met. Thank you for your unwavering encouragement and support. P.S. Your mom is really hot.

To Jennifer Haymore. This series simply would not exist without you. Thank you for believing in me. I'm sending Lucky and the MacKinnon boys to your house for a group hug. Be ready.

To Rebekah Weatherspoon, Becky Condit, and all the amazing reviewers, authors, and bloggers who've helped spread the word about my books. You do so much for the romance community. You've done so much for me. A million thanks. A special high five to Tiffany at Read All the Romance and Amber at Wicked Good Reads. I hope you both enjoy Harmony's story!

To my husband, Brent, who tells me I don't snore even though I'm pretty sure I do. I love you.

And most of all...to every girl who just wants to get lucky and isn't afraid to admit it. This one's for you.

THE NOD

"Sometimes the thing you throw away becomes the thing you most desire."
—Gabrielle Hamilton

Harmony Santos put down her fork with a clink. "Wait a second. Are you breaking up with me? On my *birthday?*"

Dr. Franklin Walker Vallejo Lockwood had so many names, she couldn't keep track of them. He was Dr. Lockwood to their patients at Bakersfield General Hospital. To the other surgical nurses in their ward, he was Dr. Dreamboat. To his wealthy, doting parents, he was Franklin, beloved only child. To Harmony, he was simply Frank, her boyfriend of almost a year.

In the candlelight, Frank looked up at her with those bright green eyes and said, "I don't think this is working out, Harm."

"What do you mean?" She was genuinely confused. "We're working out great."

"Just hear me out."

He had prepared a list of vague reasons, but Harmony was too tied up in her shock to understand anything coming out of his mouth.

This wasn't supposed to happen.

When Dr. Dreamboat finally asked her out after she'd crushed on him for months, Harmony believed her love life had come to a happy crescendo. Cue rainbows. Puppies. Blue skies. They'd been together almost a year. In good time, Harmony Santos, R.N. was certain she'd become Mrs. Harmony Santos-Lockwood, wife of the crown prince of Bakersfield.

This was no daydream. Over the last year, she'd worked her ass off to become the kind of woman worthy of this relationship. Taking her cues from Frank, she'd stopped partying and raising Cain. She learned to curb her impulsive temper, something that often got her in trouble when she was younger. Frank had complimented her on her improvements. These days, far as Harmony could see, they were the perfect couple. Doctor and nurse. Proper prince and princess. Happily ever after, forever and ever.

But now?

Still unable to grasp the meaning of his words, Harmony watched his face as he spoke. He looked sorry—the quintessential sorry person, sweet and sincere. Dr. Dreamboat did even awkward things like dumping his girlfriend on her birthday appear easy.

Rage. Confusion. Hurt. Heartache. Too many emotions to keep bottled up at once—Harmony panicked. She had to get the hell out of here.

While he was in midsentence, she stood up, opened her purse, and dropped some money on the table.

"Baby, don't do that." Frank glanced down at the bills and back up at her. "Where are you going?"

"Home. I'm going home." Keeping her face still, Harmony turned and walked out of the fancy restaurant.

Trembling, she called her older sister from the highway. Melody picked up right away. "Hey, birthday girl. What's up?"

The words came out on their own. "I'm coming down."

"Why? What's wrong?"

Tears welled in Harmony's eyes, but she forced herself not to cry. *No blubbering.* She made her voice hard and clear. "Frank—he dumped me. Tonight."

"Oh, crap." Melody fell quiet. Harmony heard the muffled voice of her brother-in-law asking a question. "My sister's boyfriend just broke up with her. Yeah. On her birthday." Melody turned back to the phone. "Listen, we're not at home right now."

"What?" Now panic swirled inside her along with all those other messy emotions. Harmony didn't trust herself tonight, alone in her apartment with her freshly broken heart. "Where are you guys?"

"We're driving to the Silver Spur."

"The Spur?" Harmony sniffed. "Tonight? Why?"

"Tonight's the grand reopening. Come meet us there."

Someone grabbed the phone. "Harm? This is Clark. Forget that prick and get your cowgirl ass to Oleander." A series of deep whoops and hollers sounded in the background. His brothers and their girls were with him—instant party.

Harmony blinked. Noise, drinking, dancing, and her crazy patched-together family—she hadn't been out in ages. This sounded like just the ticket out of Shitsville. "All right," she said. "I'm coming."

Melody got back on the line. "See you soon, girl."

―❦―

ONE-AND-A-HALF HOURS LATER, her jumbled-up feelings in check, Harmony climbed out of her Jeep into a parking lot jam-packed with pickup trucks. She took a deep breath—warm summer air, sagebrush, and cow funk. The smell of Oleander. The smell of home.

She gave herself a once-over—black mini-dress from her date, beat-up cowboy boots she'd had in the car—and made a beeline for the crowd of people standing outside the Silver Spur, the newly remodeled cowboy bar where she had spent many an hour of her degenerate youth.

But *this*—this wasn't the rundown honky-tonk she remembered.

This was a gleaming, two-story cowboy palace. Its log-cabin exterior was lit up with strings of white lights and planted out with drought-resistant landscaping. Harmony stood gawking at the joint until her sister texted her.

I'm standing by the bouncer.

Melody wore Daisy Dukes, a glittery tank top, and brand-new cowboy boots. Her hair was curled and eyeliner accentuated her beautiful brown eyes. When Harmony hugged her big sister, an enormous wave of relief washed over her. She was home—and she might be able to salvage this horrible night.

"Look at you, gorgeous." Harmony squinted at Melody. "Hey, what's that?" She lifted her sister's hair off her neck. There was a small purple mark just beneath her earlobe.

Melody flipped her hair back to cover the hickey. "It's nothing."

Harmony rolled her eyes. "Can't that boy keep his hands off you?"

"Not really. Come on."

A big bouncer removed the velvet rope from the entrance and let them cut in front of the line. As soon as she saw the scene inside the new Silver Spur, Harmony knew she was right to leave Bakersfield behind tonight.

The original Silver Spur had been a stalwart but rather nasty piece of Oleander's history, a place for beer bottles, fists, and ugly faces to get acquainted. When Harmony first snuck into the Spur, she was seventeen years old. That was seven years ago. The only decorations in the place had been dusty beer signs and a distinguished group of grizzled locals.

But this—this was nothing like the old Spur. Owner Tom Shelton had built a flashy country-western nightclub. A long bar lined the back wall, manned by an army of sexy bartenders in cowboy hats slinging up beers and shots. A stone wall and a big fireplace lined another wall. Around the enormous sunken dance floor was a brass rail where patrons could lean, chat, and check out everyone else's dance moves. Doors led to vast smoking patios. And up front, under what looked like a mirrored disco saddle, was a big stage bathed in purple light and covered with dancers. A DJ stood in the booth on the edge of the dance floor, spinning boot-scootin' country music to the enthusiastic crowd.

"Holy moly, Mel," Harmony said. "Tom did this?"

Melody stood close enough to speak directly into Harmony's ear over the sound of the music. "He knocked the old place down and rebuilt it from the ground up. He's got musical acts booked up almost two years in advance. Big names too. He knows a lot of promoters. We're going to have tons of bands coming through here. It'll be a blast."

"I can't believe it." She looked up at the big, ornate chandeliers made of antlers. "Where will I throw up at the end of the night?"

Her sister snorted. "Not in here. Tom will blacklist you."

"We could throw up anywhere we wanted in the old place."

"It's a new day, Harm."

She followed her sister to a large, circular banquette just to the left of the stage. Some familiar faces sat in the shadows, drinking beer and talking—Melody's in-laws, the MacKinnons, old family friends. Melody's husband Clark sat on the end. Melody went to him right away and sat in his lap. They were so damn cute that Harmony wanted to throw up a little—in her mouth, so she wouldn't get in trouble with Tom.

"Happy birthday, stranger," Clark said. "Glad you came out."

Harmony bent and kissed her handsome brother-in-law on the cheek. "Hey, doofus."

"We'll kick his ass for you. Just say the word."

"I'll keep that in mind." She said hello to the other two folks at the table, Clark's brother Daniel MacKinnon and his wife Georgia, on a rare night out from their four kids. Georgia was wearing a red dress. Daniel couldn't keep his eyes off her.

"Too much lovey-dovey in this booth," Harmony whispered to her sister. "I'm going to get a drink. You want anything?"

Melody shook her head as Clark leaned forward and kissed her neck.

Harmony walked through the crowd. The room was steamy with dancing and pheromones. Harmony ordered a Bud Light and ran the icy bottle over her forehead.

As she stood at the brass rail and checked out the dancers, she recognized a handful of childhood friends and old nursing-school classmates in the arms of their boyfriends or boyfriends-for-the-night. Old-timers took their turns on the dance floor, the smoothest dancers of all. Near the front of the stage, she spotted Dean, the eldest MacKinnon brother, dancing sexy with his wife Monica. They looked unspeakably happy. Everyone did. With a grimace, Harmony killed her beer and left the bottle on a nearby tray.

A sense of misery crept over her, clinging to her like a big, wet monkey. She hated that Frank had hurt her. But even worse, she hated that she'd allowed herself to be vulnerable enough for him to do that. After months of pining followed by months of self-improvement, she'd finally gotten the man she wanted.

Trouble was, he didn't want her.

Harmony winced. *Goddammit. This pain.*

A new song started up. Shaking off her melancholy, she strode right into the heart of the crowded dance floor. Steve Earle's "Copperhead Road"—an easy line dance. She counted her way in and soon was stomping across the dance floor. The loud music pounded in her chest. Even though it had been years since she'd line danced, her body knew the steps without her thinking about them. The heartache receded a little.

More dancing. Maybe some shots. Maybe making out with a stranger. That'll keep me from feeling...this. Whatever this ugly feeling is.

She danced solo for three more songs. Then an old-timer led her in a waltz. The country gentleman was followed by a baby-faced cowboy in a camo baseball cap. She danced three more songs with him and bid him goodbye with a hug and a kiss on the cheek—too young.

The DJ took the mike. "Next up, the cowboy cha-cha."

A slower dance. Harmony fanned herself with her hand and thought this might be a good time to grab a shot of Fireball chased with another beer.

She turned to leave the dance floor when a big warm hand rested on her shoulder.

"Wait. Don't go yet."

She turned. In the dark, the new cowboy's face was obscured in the shadow of his hat. The DJ cued up an old Bellamy Brothers song Harmony remembered her father loved. It began, "If I said you had a beautiful body would you hold it against me?" She knew the words as surely as she knew her own name.

The dancers around them paired off in a hurry and got into the sweetheart position. Everyone counted off together and started around the massive dance floor in a counter-clockwise direction, all in time.

Before Harmony could say anything, the stranger took her hands and spun her. His movements were sure and strong. He was an experienced dancer, not someone who had to be babysat around the floor.

"Been a long time, hasn't it?" he said.

She stole sideways glances at him. Tall and muscular, he wore a black hat and a plaid shirt with the sleeves rolled up. His forearms were thick and smooth. She could see that he had a strong jaw, a dark, short beard, and dark skin. He spoke crystal-clear English with a lilting Mexican accent.

"You don't remember me, do you, Harmony?"

She stared.

A half-smile. "Guess I'm just another cowboy to you."

For strangers, they moved in perfect rhythm. Harmony felt grateful that he was a strong lead since her brain was otherwise occupied with trying to figure out who he was. When he brought their bodies together, chest to chest, she looked up at him. His body gave off controlled strength and a smooth, unnerving calm. At last, she peeked under the shadow of his cowboy hat.

Dark brows. Bedroom eyes the color of whiskey.

No way. "Lucky?"

Lucio "Lucky" Garcia had gone to Harmony's high school and worked as a ranch hand for the MacKinnons. She'd always known who he was, but they were never friends. Two years ago, before Harmony had left for Bakersfield, she and Lucky shared one freaky, drunken make-out session at her graduation party. For days afterward, Lucky followed her around like a puppy. After he'd helped her move to her new apartment, she'd given him a kiss on the cheek and promised to call him. But fate had different plans. That Monday, she started working at the hospital. Dr. Dreamboat entered her romantic crosshairs and she immediately forgot the existence of other men.

The Lucky of her memory was a boyish flyweight. At the time, he was still living at home with his mom. Sweet as candy, he was enthusiastic and optimistic. Everything about him screamed inexperience, sexual and otherwise.

Disoriented, Harmony stared up at her partner. The Lucky she remembered was nothing like the Lucky who held her in his arms tonight. His movements were sure as he led her around the dance floor, anticipating her every step. And he'd put on lots of muscle. His broad arms and shoulders strained against his shirt, and when he turned, she saw that his back narrowed into a tight V in Wranglers wrapped around a sexy, meaty ass. Harmony tried not to stare. Lucky had been working out. The effects were downright breathtaking.

"You look surprised to see me."

"The MacKinnons didn't tell me you were here," she said.

"No one knows I'm here. I just got back this afternoon."

"Back from what?"

"I've been on the road."

"Doing what?"

He smiled. His lips were sensual and full. Dr. Dreamboat was handsome, but he had thin lips. Kissing him sometimes felt like making out with a mail slot.

"So you really don't remember me," Lucky said softly.

The man was sexy. And annoying. "Of course I remember you." She fluttered her eyelashes like a cartoon princess. "How could I forget? I've been watching your career, tracking your every move, wishing on a star that one day we'd meet again."

Lucky grinned. "There she is. There's the sassy Harmony I remember." He spun her again, hard. Her hair whipped around. God help her, he was a good dancer. Had they danced when they'd gotten together two years ago? She would've remembered this.

He pulled her close, his hand on her waist sure and steady. Their thighs touched, his hard, muscular one thick between her legs as they swayed. He looked down at her. The heat in his eyes surprised her. She pressed her lips together and turned away, his gaze too intense for her to meet up close.

"You never called me," he said. "Were you just using me?"

Seamlessly, the DJ faded out the Bellamy Brothers and cued up "Neon Moon" by Brooks and Dunn. The dancers on the floor altered their rhythm. Lucky picked it up without a hitch.

"You didn't like being used?" she asked.

"To be honest, I would've liked being used more. Harder." The sexy bastard grinned.

The slow song turned their movements even more liquid, more sensual. As she and Lucky made their way through the crowd, she put everything else out of her mind—the couples dancing close to them, the sharp scent of fresh paint and strong whiskey, the hungry ache rising inside her. In anticipation of her birthday date with Dr. Dreamboat, she'd laid off using her vibrator all week. Her body was primed and aching for sex. Lucky pulled her even closer against him. He smelled good. Fabric softener. Musk. Spice. His whole body was hard underneath his clothes. She struggled to keep her arousal under wraps, but he was making it extremely difficult.

"How about you, Harmony?" Her name on his lips was like a magic spell. "Do you like to be used?"

She closed her eyes. *Why does he feel so damn good?* "Sometimes."

He lowered his lips to her ear. "How about tonight? Do you want to be used tonight?"

She shivered. She would like nothing more than to lose herself tonight. She could feel the pain stalking her like a wolf in the dark, and she wanted to be numb before it got her. Numb with anything—drinking, dancing, sex. Anything to protect herself from the howling pain she knew was coming. She locked her hands behind his neck. "Dance with me. Dance with me the rest of the night."

"Then?"

"Then we'll see, cowboy."

At ten to two, the DJ announced the final song. Melody and the MacKinnons were long gone, rushed off to relieve their babysitters and hump each other senseless in bed. As promised, Lucky had gone the distance with Harmony. After hours in his arms, she was wound tight. He'd touched and handled her body until her lust was at a low, steady boil. One more slow two-step and she'd lose her mind completely, drag him into the shadows, and take him here and now.

They were sweating, having danced without a break for three hours. When the song ended, he brushed her hair back off her neck and a cool, cigarette-scented cross breeze kissed her damp skin.

"You're tense as hell," he said.

You don't know the half of it. She was wet everywhere—particularly between her legs, where she'd been slick for hours. "Where are you staying?"

"My mom's house," he said.

Two years later. Same story. He was twenty-six and still lived with his mother.

"How about you?" he asked.

"The old bunkhouse at the ranch. Melody made up a bed for me."

He brushed his lips across her temple, sending a hot shiver up her spine. "Is there room for me in that bed?"

The last song ended and the house lights went up. In the back of the room, Tom Shelton and his bartenders popped a bottle of champagne and sprayed it all over the bar while the waitresses laughed and cheered.

Should she bring Lucky home? She hadn't done anything this impulsive in a long, long time.

In the bright light from the chandeliers, Lucky was even handsomer. He took off his hat and fanned himself. His black hair was thick and wavy.

What the hell. Harmony's legs and feet ached, but she was wired. And her broken heart wouldn't catch up with her tonight if she had this hot cowboy to ride.

"All right." She took his hand and headed for the exit. "Let's go."

WHEN SHE AND Lucky arrived at MacKinnon Ranch, all the buildings were dark. Harmony's father had been ranch foreman for the MacKinnons for many years until he died unexpectedly when she was very young. She'd grown up on this ranch and knew it inside and out. While Lucky stroked the back of her neck, she drove her Jeep down one of the dirt roads to the bunkhouse two klicks from the main farmhouse, parked it, and killed the engine.

"Come on," she whispered.

They were giddy and horny, but neither had been drinking beyond Harmony's initial beer. If it were possible, she was high on Lucky.

They stumbled across the yard to the bunkhouse. Sixty years ago, it had been used by the itinerant cowboys who did seasonal work on the ranch. These days it sat vacant.

She opened the door. Rows of empty bunk beds sat along the walls, their mattresses removed. In the corner was a big double bed, made up with fresh linens. Melody had set up a reading lamp and an electric fan on a small table. The room was surprisingly cool.

After exchanging a mischievous glance, Harmony and Lucky raced each other to the bed. Lucky caught her before she could get to it, hoisted her over his shoulder, and tossed her onto the mattress.

And then he was on top of her.

"Kiss me," she whispered.

At last those warm, sensual lips were on hers. Harmony kissed him hungrily, letting his heat spread through her until every part of her tingled. Soon she was so hot she couldn't breathe. She knocked the hat off his head and plunged her hands through his damp, thick hair, dragging him down deeper into the kiss. His short beard brushed her chin, sharpening her sense of touch. When he slid his thick tongue between her teeth, she licked him back, beckoning him deeper. He tasted sweet, like cinnamon chewing gum. Heat, rhythm, pressure—no denying it. The man could kiss as well as he could dance, and he was a fucking amazing dancer.

Could he kiss like this before? I would've remembered this.

After a long, hot make-out session that left her trembling, Lucky broke their kiss and began to undress her. Together they yanked off her boots. She sat up as he pulled her dress over her head. When he saw the barely-there bra and thong she wore underneath, Lucky looked back up at her, his eyes on fire.

"I can't believe you've been wearing those all night."

"What did you think I was wearing?"

"I don't know. Not *that*."

Still staring at her body, he stood up, unbuttoned his shirt, and dropped it on the floor. His white undershirt clung to his muscular body for dear life, the cotton straining against his shoulders. Harmony clenched her thighs together, anticipation pounding in her bloodstream.

She bit her lip and stared up at him. He was hotter than the devil's asscrack. Wild-eyed, jacked, bearded—a shaggy-haired double dose of cowboy sex on legs. He was the complete opposite of cool, urbane Frank.

Stop—stop thinking of Frank.

"Take off your clothes," she said abruptly.

Lucky cocked an eyebrow at her as he untucked his under-shirt. "In a hurry?"

"I didn't say talk."

He pulled the thin cotton shirt over his head. Harmony took a deep breath. He smelled unbelievably good: soap, musk, sweat. In the lamplight, her eyes feasted on the sight of his shirtless body. Golden-brown skin, hard rounded pecs crowned with tiny brown nipples, just a whisper of dark chest hair. Her eyes slid down his torso. Sharply defined abs and a shallow belly button. Deep indentations marked the tops of his hips and disappeared into his black jeans. He radiated controlled calm.

She held out her arms. "Come here."

Quickly, he yanked off his boots and socks and climbed onto the bed, cradling the back of her head with his big hands as he kissed her again and again. She slid her palms slowly up and down his hard, hot back, her fingertips exploring the swells and hollows of muscle. Between kisses, he smiled and looked her in the eye, hypnotizing her. He fitted his body tightly against hers, his hips pinning hers to the old mattress.

"Two years ago…I wanted you to call me," he whispered against her lips. He stroked her hair. "I wanted you so much."

His hot gaze was so direct she could feel him getting under her skin—somewhere he did not belong, not tonight. She tipped her chin up and gave him another kiss, biting his sweet bottom lip and scraping gently it with her teeth. "We're here now," she said.

With a grin, he lifted her up and snapped off her bra with a quick flick of his fingers. He pulled it from her body and stared at her, his eyes glittering with heat. He placed his warm hands on her breasts and kneaded them, his perfect sense of touch and pressure sending sharp spikes of pleasure up her spine. He lowered his lips to hers and kissed her again, feasting on her as his rough thumbs stroked her tender nipples. She arched her back, longing for more. He plunged his tongue into her mouth as he pinched her nipples—softly at first, then increasingly rougher as she responded to him, moaning like a wild woman under his spell.

Goose bumps broke out over her body when he released her tingling lips at last. After laying a line of openmouthed kisses down her throat, he suddenly sucked one of her nipples into his hot mouth. Strumming the tip with his tongue, Lucky massaged her other nipple with his fingertips, firing up her nerves and making her addled brain wonder if he could make her come with nothing more than a skillful session of nipple play. As she stroked the hard planes of his shoulders and ran her fingers through his hair, Harmony realized she hadn't felt this turned on in months. Lucky was a sensualist, an explorer just like her. Frank was different—in bed, he was all business, eyes on the prize.

Stop thinking about Frank.

Harmony opened her eyes. The small reading lamp cast strange shadows on the bare rafters of the bunkhouse. *This fucking heartache.* Hiding up in those shadows, it was breathing, waiting—the wolf was coming to get her. She needed to protect herself from it. She needed the numbness that only Lucky could give her tonight. She took his hand and plucked it from her breast. He released her nipple and looked into her face as she slid his hand down her stomach to her panties.

"What's the rush?" The deep timbre of his voice penetrated her chest.

"I need it," she said breathlessly. "Please."

She examined his face. What was it about him that made her feel unhinged? Those cheekbones, those full lips, his slow smile. "Okay. If that's what you need."

He was breathing hard. Even in the faint light, she could see the generous outline of his erection behind his fly. He got to his knees on the mattress, put his hands on her thighs and gently drew them apart. His gaze rested between her legs and lingered there. She'd gotten waxed. She was wearing a peach lace thong with a gossamer-thin mesh panel. Lucky's dark eyes narrowed, zeroing in on her.

"So pretty," he whispered.

He lay down between her legs and rested his weight on his forearms. His warm breath caressed her inner thighs, and antici-pation boiled like hot syrup in her veins. When Lucky hooked his big finger around her thong and pulled it to the side, exposing her, cool air from the electric fan kissed her pussy. She propped herself up on her elbows and looked down at him. They locked eyes.

"I'm going to make you regret not calling me." He ran the pad of his thumb slowly along her hot, slick pussy lips, resting with a featherweight touch on her aching clit.

Harmony threw her head back and closed her eyes. "Yes."

Lucky took his time. With his fingertips, he caressed her aching flesh with a rhythmic sensuality that made Harmony's breath catch in her throat. Slowly, he stroked her into a dream state, stirring her nerve endings until they hummed under his touch. When she opened her eyes, she saw that he was staring at her pussy, heavy-lidded eyes transfixed, lips parted. He was studying her and learning her responses. Focused on her pleasure, he'd quickly learned the parts of her that were more sensitive than the others and spent more time touching her there. He slid a finger into her aching opening and drew it out slowly, spreading her arousal all over and swirling it hotly on her clit. She whimpered and he did it again. He repeated the movement a half-dozen times. Harmony's body clenched tight with desire.

Still holding her panties off to the side, Lucky lowered his lips to her clit and kissed it as he plunged two fingers into her. Electrical pulses fired in her brain. He crossed her wires—pain and pleasure at once, each sensation intensifying the other.

He'd been touching her all night, beginning with the moment he'd put his hand on her shoulder. After hours of foreplay, on the dance floor and now here in bed, Harmony was out of her mind. His lips stayed sealed to her as his tongue strummed her clit, up and down. He fucked her hard with his fingers. The wet, raunchy sound filled her ears as her own liquid dripped down her asscrack onto the sheets.

She grabbed the covers in her fists. "Lucky." Her whisper was ragged. "I'm going to come."

He didn't stop. He worked her hard with his tongue and fingers, his rhythm steady. His beard abraded her tender skin, heightening her pleasure. When the first wild flutters of her orgasm exploded deep inside her, Harmony shut her eyes. Her entire lower body seized up. Her pussy contracted hard against his fingers but he kept banging her, and he didn't stop licking even when her back bent into a high arch. She grabbed his head and rode his tongue as the orgasm tore out of her, feral and free. Blood pounded in her ears. She hadn't come this hard in months.

Before she caught her breath, Lucky pulled back and slid out of her. With lightning speed, he unbuckled his belt and pulled down his fly. He yanked his pants and boxers down his muscular thighs. Before Harmony had a chance to ogle him, he'd rolled on a condom and fitted himself between her legs, the broad head of his cock nudging her trembling, swollen pussy.

He lowered himself carefully over her, pressing his hard chest against her.

"Kiss me." He slid his hands underneath her head again, cradling her, making her feel safe.

She fell headlong into his wild brown eyes and drowned in another searing kiss. She dug her hands through his hair and arched against him, needing more. Her overheated body trembled, exposed and raw from her enormous climax.

Lucky broke their kiss. Under his piercing gaze, she had nowhere to hide and nowhere to run.

"Ready?" His voice was a warm whisper against her lips.

She wrapped her arms around his solid shoulders and nodded.

Eyes never leaving hers, Lucky snapped his hips forward and buried his long, thick cock inside her.

God, yes.

He felt so good that Harmony's eyes watered. She spread her legs wider as he thrust deep. His cool balls rested gently against her ass. Eyes still open, he kissed her again and again, his tongue slowly exploring her mouth as he dug into her with his cock. Intimacy blended with an overload of sensation, leaving Harmony raw and vulnerable. Body and soul aching, she let him in. His weight and heat overwhelmed her, but every part of her cried out for more.

He pulled back and thrust into her again, tapping some tender place inside her that had never been touched. Harmony closed her eyes. She couldn't hold back. Lucky broke their kiss and ran his lips lightly over her cheeks, tasting her tears.

"Am I hurting you?"

She buried her face against his neck. "No. Keep going."

"Are you sure?"

"I'm sure. Please, Lucky. Don't stop."

He kissed her lips once more, planted his hands on the mattress, and lifted himself a few inches above her. As he looked down at her, his face was full of dark, sensual promise.

"Harmony," he said. "Touch yourself. Touch yourself, while I make love to you."

She blinked. *Love. That stupid word.* She wiped her tears away and ran her fingers over his lips. He licked them. His tongue was hot.

"We're not making love," she whispered.

He gave her a crooked grin and another thrust. "We're not?"

"No." With her wet fingers, she reached down between them and touched her swollen clit. She was already on the edge of another big orgasm.

"What are we doing, then?"

"You know what we're doing."

With that, Lucky leaned back on his legs and put his hands on her hips. Still stroking herself, Harmony stared at his glistening chest. He was panting hard; the muscles in his torso flexed lightly with each breath. He was staring at her too. The heat of his gaze seared her skin. He pressed his lips together. Eyes locked on hers, he gave her another delicious thrust, then another. He adjusted his grip and lifted her ass off the bed. Mesmerized, Harmony slid her free hand over his sweat-slick abs and watched his calm face as he fucked her. His thrusts were deep and controlled, perfectly in sync with the bottomless cravings of her body.

After a dozen strokes, he squeezed her hips and closed his eyes. He let his head hang back. Harmony looked at the muscles and tendons in his neck, the outline of his Adam's apple in the shadows.

"God," he murmured. "You feel amazing."

She rubbed herself hard but eased up each time she got too close, denying herself a climax through another dozen strokes. She was sweating by the time he reached forward and gripped her breasts. He wasn't gentle, but the sensation of his rough hands on her made her even wetter. When he opened his eyes again, her entire body was on fire and aching for release.

With a grunt, he slid his hands behind her knees and pushed her legs as far apart as they could go. Splayed open, her fingers on her hard little clit, Harmony was a heartbeat away from falling apart.

"I'm close," she whispered.

"Do it."

Lucky pressed his big cock deep into her and held it there. He flexed his abs, pushing the head of his cock against the front wall of her pussy, and she exploded at once. He smiled as a second colossal orgasm rolled over her like thunder, destroying her with pleasure.

She still was dazed when, a few seconds later, he pulled out of her, flipped her over, and lifted her until she was on all fours in front of him. Without a word, he thrust into her again, his fingers digging into her hips as he smacked his rock-hard abs against her ass. He reached forward and fingered her tender clit. Harmony flinched, still raw from two orgasms.

"You're going to come again for me, aren't you?"

"I can't," she said, her voice a broken whisper.

"You can."

His cock was rigid and thick as a lodgepole pine inside her. He fucked her relentlessly. This wasn't the polite, businesslike sex Frank liked. This was something else entirely. Lucky was messing with her brain, making her rethink what she knew and understood about her body.

With his other hand, he swept the hair off her neck, leaned down, and kissed her nape. Harmony closed her eyes, gripping the iron headboard of the ancient bed for dear life. She didn't understand what he was doing to her, but she was on fire. When he leaned forward and changed his angle inside her, something insane happened—the promise of a third orgasm shimmered deep inside her.

She dripped down onto the pillows—tears or sweat, she wasn't sure. "What are you doing to me?" she whispered.

His deep voice was smooth and devilish in her ear. "You know what I'm doing to you."

He gathered her hair in his fist while his other hand played a symphony on her clitoris. When he pulled her head back, Harmony lost all control of her body. Screaming, she came again —a third long, wet orgasm, all over his cock. He gave her five more wild strokes and caught the tail end of her climax with his. When he groaned, every muscle in his glorious body flexed. Still in the haze of her own release, she could feel the hot pulses running through his body. With a crushing grip, he held on to her and together they rode his orgasm out to the last shudder.

Breathless, she collapsed onto the pillows as he pulled gently out of her. After another soft kiss on the back of her shoulder, he left the bed to clean up. When he sat down on the bed and stroked her hair, she closed her eyes. His touch was tender—at odds with what they'd just done. Before she could stop herself, a deep sob escaped her lips.

"Oh, God," she whispered.

Lucky took her hand. "Harmony, did I hurt you? What's wrong?"

She looked up at him. Her dark lover had turned into a gentle protector in a heartbeat. "No. You didn't hurt me. It's not you." She sat up and buried her face in her hands. She was a hot mess.

He didn't need to see this. No one needed to see this. "I'm sorry. I'm so sorry."

He stroked her cheek. "Sorry for what?"

The tears fell freely now. "It's just..." She trailed off.

"Hey." He took her in his arms at once. "Easy."

Just like he had on the dance floor, Lucky held her close to his chest, wrapped up in his strength. Harmony was not a shrinking violet. She was closer to the ogre in a fairy tale than the damsel in distress. But Lucky was so much bigger than her that she allowed herself to lean against him, drawing strength from his steadiness.

"You're not going to like this." She sniffled. "I know I wouldn't."

"What is it?"

Shame swirled in Harmony's stomach along with all the melancholy Dr. Dreamboat had left there earlier in the evening. So much for her plan to outrun her sadness. She took a deep breath and spit out the truth. "My boyfriend dumped me. Tonight."

Lucky froze. "Tonight?"

"Yes." She winced. As far as awkward situations went, this was way up there. Why did she have to tell him anything? Why couldn't this have been what she'd planned—a night of meaningless sex to dull the pain? What was it about Lucky that made her tell him the truth? "We broke up over dinner. I drove here to see my sister. I just wanted to dance. Get drunk. Lose myself."

He pulled away from her. Harmony braced herself for his anger.

"Did you love him?" he asked.

That wasn't what she'd expected him to say. She blinked. "Yes." *I think I did.*

Lucky said nothing for a moment. He touched his fingertips to her lips and trailed them down her throat. He pressed his big hand against her left breast. "Is your heart broken?"

Lucky's unexpected gesture called attention to the cold, deep ache in her chest. Again, she told him the truth. "Yes."

He dropped his hand. "So you were just using me? Again?"

"Yes." More shame. Harmony looked down at her hands. "God, what a coldhearted monster."

"True." He sighed. "But not coldhearted. Brokenhearted. That's different." He pulled her into another embrace. She sobbed against his bare chest. "Go ahead. Cry. It's natural. Let it out."

At last, Harmony let herself go. She hadn't cried in years, and this was not an ugly cry. This was a hideous openmouthed cry, replete with plenty of snot and braying.

When she choked out her last sobs, Lucky wiped her tears and boogers away with his undershirt. She blinked at him. In the lamplight, with his dark disheveled hair and beard, he looked like a big, sexy bear who just so happened to be hanging out in her bed.

"I'm sorry I used you," she said softly.

He let her go and stood up. "I forgive you." He straightened the covers, turned off the light and climbed in next to her. "And I got something pretty good out of it, so don't feel too bad." He pulled the sheets over both of them and wrapped his big arms around her again.

"Lucky—"

"Shh."

"But—"

"Three times and you still have energy to talk?" He paused. "Do I have to fuck you again?"

In spite of herself, she smiled. It was the first time he'd said the word aloud tonight. "Good night, Lucky."

He held her tightly in his heavy arms. "Good night."

Harmony scanned the dark bunkhouse, its spooky interior haunted by shadows. In a few minutes, Lucky's breathing grew deep and even. Before long he was snoring softly in her ear, his body wrapped around hers like armor against her loneliness.

Exhausted inside and out, she closed her eyes and fell asleep at last.

—◇—

HARMONY WOKE UP ALONE. Lucky was gone. Sore in the best way possible, she got up and showered in the bunkhouse bathroom. Her detail-oriented older sister had left her some clean clothes. She changed into a T-shirt and jeans and put her boots back on. The walk to the farmhouse got her blood going. She said hello to a couple of ranch hands doing their chores. The early-morning air was already warm.

She wiped her feet on the mat outside the back door and entered the MacKinnons' mudroom. Three friendly Aussie shepherds greeted her with wags and nose-nudges. She petted them and walked into the kitchen.

At the stove, Georgia was dressed for work on the ranch. She carried her two-year-old daughter on her hip. The little one was pulling on her mother's braids as she watched Georgia stir up a big pot of oatmeal one-handed. Harmony kissed Georgia on the cheek as the rest of Georgia's kids came to sit at the big table, followed by their grandmother Cecilia "Cece" MacKinnon, who poured herself the first of many cups of coffee.

Harmony gave her a big hug. "Auntie Cece."

The little brown-haired woman was spunky and energetic as ever. "Oh, honey! It's been so long since we've seen you! How's everything going? How's work? And your handsome doctor friend?"

Georgia looked wide-eyed at Cece and made a throat-slitting motion with her free hand. "Ix-nay on the oyfriend-bay."

Cece clapped a hand over her mouth. "Ix-nay on the—oh! I see. Forget I said anything. Coffee?" She smiled goofily as she poured Harmony another cup.

"Thank you." Harmony accepted the cup and let it warm her

hands. As she took her first sip, she swore all operations on MacKinnon Ranch would come to a grinding halt if that coffeemaker ever broke down.

Harmony took over cooking while Cece and Georgia got all the big kids fed, packed up, and sent to the bus stop on time. Daniel came through the back door, kissed Georgia, and took the baby from her. He strapped the little girl into her high chair as Melody came downstairs. Dean walked in through the front door, holding his six-month-old son Dale in a baby carrier. A huge yellow diaper bag covered in ducklings was slung over his shoulder. He was helping on the ranch for the day, but he and his wife Monica lived in town, where she worked at the chamber of commerce and kept the books for her family's many businesses.

The controlled chaos of the MacKinnon household fell into order as everyone took a seat at the breakfast table. At the head of the table was an empty place set for Dale MacKinnon, Cece's husband, who'd passed away a year earlier. He'd left a big hole in their lives. Harmony still missed him. They all did.

The table was set and Cece was about to say a prayer when the front door opened. In walked Clark and Lucky.

"Sit down, guys," Melody called. "We're about to start."

The two men quickly took their seats. Lucky took the empty chair next to Harmony and greeted her with a half-smile. He was wearing his clothes from the night before.

"Morning," he said softly.

Harmony's face flushed in spite of herself. Everyone was staring at them. "Morning."

The babies babbled quietly through Cece's quick prayer. She thanked God for the food and for her family, and for the guests Harmony and Lucky. She asked Jesus to look after Dale and Harmony and Melody's parents too.

Amen was followed by pancakes, bacon, eggs, and oatmeal. Fresh milk, good butter. Coffee, and lots of it. Between tiny cups of yogurt in her apartment and fancy dinners out with Dr.

Dreamboat, it had been too long since Harmony enjoyed a home-cooked meal. Ravenous, she and Lucky put away piles of food. Melody made eye contact with Harmony and winked. Harmony frowned at her, reaching for more bacon.

"So Lucky, where's the next show?" Dean asked.

Lucky took a drink of coffee. "Payson. Couple of weeks."

"Payson?" Harmony asked.

"Arizona. That's a big rodeo," said Clark. "Didn't he tell you? Lucky might make world finals for tie-down roping this year."

"Payson's my last chance to qualify."

"Who are your sponsors now?" asked Dean. "You've got Walker Ranch, Scout Tools, and Yamamoto, right?"

"Plus the Chevy dealership," Lucky said, his mouth half full. He swallowed. "They signed on late last season."

"As much as we miss having you on the ranch, I'm so proud of you, Lucky. So proud," said Cece. "And your brother in college too. Your mom must be so happy. "

"She's happy about Abel. As for me, standings change so quickly, it's hard to say if I'll make the cut."

"Still, that is something, Luck." Dean nodded to himself. "Whatever the case, you ought to be proud of yourself."

"Do you miss it, Dean?" Lucky asked. "Being on the road?"

Before Dean could answer, his son snuffled, grimaced, and took a deep breath. "Here it comes," Dean said. Two seconds later, the baby let out a wail like the siren on a fire truck. Dean lowered his face and sniffed the kid. He put his spoon down, picked up the carrier and diaper bag, and headed for the bathroom. "'Scuse me."

When Dean was gone, Cece turned to Harmony. "A little birdie told me something."

Melody stood up and stuck a pink candle in the remaining pancakes on Harmony's plate. Clark struck a match and lit it. "Happy birthday, troublemaker," he said.

As they sang to her, just like they used to when she was a

child, Harmony looked at all of their smiling faces. She and Melody had grown up with the MacKinnon boys. It was comforting to know they'd always have her back if she ever needed help. And it made her happy to see them starting families and living lives of their own.

She blew out the candle with a lighter heart.

After breakfast, many hands made light work of clearing the table and cleaning the kitchen. Cece took over watching the babies while everyone else went to work on the ranch. Lucky followed Harmony out of the house.

"Can you give me a ride home?" he asked.

"Sure."

Together they walked back to her Jeep. "I didn't know it was your birthday," he said. "How old are you?"

"It was yesterday. I'm twenty-five." It sounded so grown up. But she was in no better position to understand her mess of a life or the jumble of emotions inside her.

"Your boyfriend broke up with you on your birthday? What a dickhead."

"Let's not talk about that." She waved her hand. "Tell me about Payson. That sounds really cool, Lucky."

He shrugged, grinning. "I've been roping since I was eighteen. This is the closest I've ever come to qualifying for world finals. I still can't believe it."

"It's been years since I've been to the rodeo. How does tie-down roping work?"

"It's a timed event. A calf runs into the arena. When it reaches a certain point, the horse and rider chase after it. The rider ropes the calf, dismounts, lifts the calf, ties three of its legs together, and throws up his hands to stop the clock."

"How long do you have?"

"A good time is nine seconds."

"Jesus."

"After that, the calf has to stay tied for six seconds. If it does, then that time is recorded. If not, the whole run doesn't count. That's it. Speed is key. Having a good horse is important."

"What's your horse's name?"

"Batman."

"Does he look like Batman?"

Lucky shook his head. "No. I just like the name Batman."

"Goofball." She smiled. "Are your sister and mother going to cheer you on?"

He shook his head again. "I was saving for them to come to Arizona. But Abel's laptop broke a few weeks ago. We used the money to buy him a new one."

"That's too bad."

"I really wanted them to go, but the computer was more important." They walked in silence for a little while. Lucky cleared his throat. "Tell me something."

"What?"

"Are you going to call him again?"

"Who?"

"Your ex."

Harmony stuck her hands in her pockets. If she were smart, she'd let it go. Before she could answer Lucky's question, Clark and Daniel drove by them in the Gator, one of the dogs sitting in the back.

"See you later, you crazy kids," Daniel called, waving at them.

Clark sang, "Lucky and Harmony sitting in a tree. Bleep-bleep-bleep-bleep-I-N-G!"

The brothers whistled and hollered as they bumped down the road. When they were out of earshot, Harmony said, "Do you think they know what we did?"

Lucky grinned. "The way we were acting last night at the Spur? They know. Of course they know."

"God." She shuddered. "They must think I'm such a slut."

"Whoa. Easy there." He looked at her. "So you broke up with your boyfriend and went home with the hottest Mexican tie-down roper in Oleander. Who cares?" He put his arm around her shoulders and pulled her close. They fell into step at once. "Sometimes the body needs what it needs. And those guys? The things they've done?" He laughed. "Trust me. They don't care. You shouldn't either."

They climbed into her Jeep and headed downtown. At the end of Main Street, Harmony turned onto a narrow side street, over an irrigation ditch and past a few low-slung houses with pickup trucks parked on the grass. She stopped in front of a bungalow at the end of the block, a small house with peeling green paint and a neat row of rosebushes by the door. In the long driveway were a rundown truck and a horse trailer with attached living quarters.

"You want to come in?" he asked. "No one's home."

She lifted an eyebrow at him. "Are you trying to get back into my jeans?"

"Maybe. Or maybe I just want you to meet my horse."

Harmony turned off her engine and climbed out. She followed Lucky around the side of the house. The building was old and needed some serious TLC, but the yard was meticulously kept. Shiny new wind chimes hung on the porch. Above the door hung a wooden plaque: *"Que en este hogar florezca el amor y la paz de Dios."*

"What does that mean?" she asked, pointing.

Lucky glanced at the plaque. "It means something like, 'May the love and peace of God—flower? Um, flourish?—in this house.'" He took her hand. "Come on."

They walked around back. A big vegetable garden was laid out in careful, precise rows of cabbage, leafy greens, and what Harmony recognized as carrot tops and beet tops. Past that, Lucky had set up a small corral with a run-in shed. A beautiful reddish-gold horse stood at the other end of the corral, tail flicking back and forth in the morning sunshine.

"Stay here." Lucky let go of her hand. He went inside the house and came out holding a couple slices of stale bread. He gave one to Harmony. "We keep these around for her. They're like horse candy. Watch."

He whistled softly and the horse's ears pricked. She walked to where he stood at the fence, reached over and plucked the bread from his hand with a loud crunch. He rubbed the side of her neck and beckoned Harmony forward. "Your turn."

Harmony held the bread out and Lucky's horse took it with another eager crunch. Her lips were warm and drooly. Harmony rubbed the horse's velvety nose. "So Batman's a girl?" she asked.

"Yes." Lucky laughed. "Batman's a girl."

"You're a strange man."

After she wiped her palm on her jeans, Lucky took her hand again. He led her to a small wooden bench under a tree by the vegetable garden. When she sat down, the fragrance of summer plums enveloped her. He reached up and plucked a ripe one from a low-hanging branch. He rinsed it with a garden hose and handed it to her. She took a bite of the ruby-red fruit, and its rich, winey sweetness filled her mouth.

"My dad planted this tree." Lucky sat down next to her, took off his hat, and ran his hand through his hair. "Right before the son of a bitch took off."

"How old were you when he left?"

"Sixteen. We'd been in the country for two years. He went back to Zacatecas. Started another family there. Forgot about us. My mother thinks he wasn't prepared for the amount of work that we had to do when we got here. He was an only son, spoiled from a young age. No stomach for shitwork." He stretched out his long legs, resting his arms on the back of the bench. "On the other hand, I have a bottomless stomach for shitwork. My mom, the same. I think we were born for it."

"What does your mother do?"

"She's a janitor. Fulltime at the middle school. She cleans motel rooms on the weekends. Before he left for college, my brother worked construction. After school, my sister works at the ice cream parlor." He kicked at the dirt with his heel. "I don't want to sound like I'm complaining. God knows we are lucky to have jobs. And we're no longer working in the fields. That was hell." He smiled sadly. "We saved all of my winnings and my brother's income to pay for his first year at school. He's only on partial scholarship. Between his tuition, the bills, putting some money away in my sister's college fund..." He trailed off. "Money's tight. Really tight."

"What are your options?"

"Rodeo—for the amount you must spend to participate, it's not a consistent paycheck. To see any kind of return on your investment, you can't just *win*, you have to be a superstar. The guys I'm competing against, they're like royalty. Their fathers, their grandfathers were world champions. It's in their blood. They have lots of support." He reached up and pulled down another plum. He polished it on his shirt and took a bite. The juice wet his bottom lip and he licked it away. "Me? I have to give it up soon. It's a luxury. Too unpredictable."

Harmony searched his face. He was proud of what he'd accomplished as a roper. He loved his horse. How could he give it all up? The decision hurt him. He hid his pain well.

"I talked to Clark this morning," Lucky continued. "They will need help on the ranch in a few months, but they don't have anything until then. I'll ask around, see what's available. Maybe look for another job in town. I don't know. My brother, we could get him through college if we economized. But Araceli will be in college in a year. With both of them in school, I don't know how we'll make it. I just don't know."

Harmony was quiet. She'd been wrong about Lucky. He wasn't a slacker kid who still lived with his mother. He was the man of the house, supporting his family.

"What does your sister want to study?" asked Harmony.

Lucky turned to her. "Actually, maybe you can help me with that."

"Help you? How?"

"Araceli is really smart. Independent. She just turned seventeen. I'm worried about her a little bit. She doesn't talk to me like she used to." He finished the plum and wiped his mouth with the back of his hand. "I know she wants to be a nurse. Would it be possible for her to spend the day at work with you sometime, just so that she can see what it's really like?"

"I'm a medical surgical nurse. Is that what she wants to do?"

"I'm not sure. I just want her to see what kind of job she can get if she studies hard. A good job, with a real salary. Not just work—a career. What do you think?"

Harmony nodded. "Sure. We can set something up."

"Excellent." Lucky stifled a yawn. "Damn. You really wore me out last night." He smiled and brushed her hair off her neck. "How about you? How do you feel?"

"A little sore." She smiled sheepishly. "Sore in a good way."

He nodded as if to say, *Of course you are.* "And your heart? Still broken?"

She looked at his big hand resting on his knee. It was rough, scarred, fingers crooked and swollen with manual labor. Pain rolled through her when she thought about Frank's surgeon's hands, the fingers neat and long. She nodded. "Yeah. Pretty much."

"Tell me. What did you like about him? What was it about him?"

She paused. "At first, I guess I was a little bit star-struck. He's a surgeon, one of the best in the state. On top of that, everyone knows the Lockwoods in Bakersfield."

"Jesus, a *Lockwood*? That is serious money."

"I've met his parents. They're really nice." She paused. "Actually, they're a little intense. Just like he is."

"What do you mean by 'intense'?"

She searched for the right words. "He knows his place in the world. He has a very clear sense of the way things are. He sizes people up quickly. Being with him helped me grow up a lot. He's a good judge of character."

"He's a shitty judge of character if he broke up with you."

God, Lucky was sweet—sweeter than the plum he'd just given her. "Maybe that's why it hurts so much." She sighed. "You know, I really thought he was the one. I had a crush on him from the moment I met him. I waited and waited. And when he asked me out, I thought I had it made."

"A crush, huh? I can understand that." Lucky's expression was unreadable. "Tell me the truth. Just between you and me, do you want him back?"

She searched the big gaping hole in her chest where the tatters of her heart still beat. "I don't know."

"Do you want to talk to him again?" Lucky asked.

Last night, Harmony had followed her impulses and run away from Frank without saying a word. Instead of staying to talk it out and find out why they'd broken up, she'd gone right back to her hell-raising ways and ended up in bed with a cowboy.

Why did she pull stunts like this? All the work she'd done to become less impulsive meant nothing. She was still the same immature person she always was on the inside. Maybe Frank was right to break up with her.

Regret, hot and bitter, bubbled in her chest. "Yeah, I should probably talk to him."

Lucky stretched out and crossed his ankles. Harmony's gaze landed on the generous bulge in his jeans before she forced herself to look away. "Since you're helping me with Araceli," he said, "maybe there's something I can do for you."

"What do you mean?"

"Back before Clark married your sister, he'd give me lessons on how to pick up women—stop laughing! It's how I got you to make out with me that one night."

Pick-up tricks? On her? Harmony shuddered. "Ugh. Please tell me that's not true."

"It is, but that's beside the point. He had this theory. 'Cat string' theory. All it means is this: people want what they can't have. Men or women, it doesn't matter. Put yourself out of someone's reach and that person will only want you more."

"Sure, but how does Clark's creepy pick-up artist trick apply to my situation?"

"Is there some kind of party or event where you'll see your ex soon?"

She thought for a moment. There was something. "One of the hospital administrators is having a retirement party at her house on Saturday night. It's a masquerade party, kind of fancy. I said I'd go. Everyone in the ward who isn't scheduled to work will be there."

"And your doctor?"

"He's off that night. He'll probably attend."

Lucky nodded. "Perfect. You're taking a date."

"A date?"

"Yes. A big sexy cowboy named Lucky Garcia. And you will witness 'cat string' theory in person."

"No! You're nuts!"

"Yes. And you're nuts too." He put his fingers under her chin and turned her face to him. "You're thinking, 'It's such a crazy idea. But it could work.' Well, don't think. Because let me tell you, nothing gets a guy's attention faster than someone else putting his hands all over what he thinks is his."

"He's not a caveman like you and Clark."

"It'll work." Lucky smirked. "Trust me."

2

PITCHING HIS SLACK

"It ain't me you're looking for, babe."
—Bob Dylan

Lucky tried to kiss Harmony when she left the house, but she dodged him with a cool smile.

"Call me," she said. "Let me know about Araceli."

She climbed into her little Jeep and waved goodbye, taking off for Bakersfield, her shiny black hair blowing in the wind.

Lucky stripped and took a hot shower, washing the scent of her off his skin. A vague sense of restlessness hummed in his bones. Making love to her had been everything he'd dreamed and more. Two years ago, he would've given anything to find himself in her bed. But she'd moved away, fading out as soon as she started her life in Bakersfield.

That heartbreak coincided with the time he got serious about roping. Bo Walker, a local stock contractor, had given Lucky a good deal on a working quarter horse with good cow sense. When Lucky first met Batman, he knew she was the one. The hundreds of hours they spent practicing together transformed them into a well-oiled team. He started to rack up local wins. They began to travel all over the country together. This season alone, they'd brought back a few thousand dollars in aggregate winnings. Add to that the incredible possibility that he might qualify for world finals? Lucky couldn't help feeling optimistic for the first time in his life.

His pockets were fat from another first-place finish when he returned from Texas the day before. He traveled on a less-than-shoestring budget, so after gas and entry fees, his winnings amounted to a little more than twelve hundred dollars. This money would go into his sister's college savings account, but not before Lucky peeled off a hundred and handed it to his mom.

They spoke Spanish at home. "Buy yourself something nice," he said. "Something pretty."

"Something pretty? Like what?"

"I don't know. Roses."

"Who needs roses, Lucio? They die." Still, she was smiling as she put the crisp bill in her pocketbook. "Thank you, *mijo*."

His sister drove him to the Silver Spur and pouted when he sent her home. "Sorry. Four more years. Then you can come in."

He'd been in the fancy nightclub for less than five minutes when he spotted Harmony in the middle of the dance floor, wrapped up in the arms of a young wannabe cowboy. She was laughing and having a good time, but judging from her body language, she was trying to extricate herself politely from the situation.

Lucky had stood like an idiot, staring at her.

In the two years since he'd seen her, she had changed. The Harmony of his memory was not the Harmony that stood before him now. She was still on the short side, but her body had filled out into a perfect hourglass. Her long hair hung like a black curtain halfway down her back. Every now and then she flicked it off her shoulder. She wore a tight dress and boots and looked like a cowboy's wet dream come true.

Good for him and his dental health, the kid let her go and bowed out. She was turning to leave when Lucky snapped out of his trance. He strode over to her and rested his hand on her shoulder.

"Wait. Don't go yet."

The night unfolded like the fantasies he used to have of her. Right there on the dance floor where everyone could see, she let him hold her. He touched her bare skin, caressed her neck, and whispered in her ear. She was such a good dancer he had trouble keeping up with her. They danced for three hours straight, and when the lights came up, he was half mad with horniness. Being so close to his long-term object of desire had short-circuited his brain.

Then they drove back to the bunkhouse, where she proceeded to blow his mind.

Lucky turned up the hot water in the shower as he thought about it. He soaped up, gripped his hard dick in his fist, and slowly began to stroke himself as he remembered everything they'd done.

In the last two years, the road had given him more education than any college class. More experienced ropers had recommended he work out to get faster and stronger, so he started lifting weights and running regularly. Not only did he shave seconds off his time, women soon responded to his changing body.

Lucky wasn't a moron. He knew that buckle bunnies chased anything that looked like a rodeo cowboy. But he found he didn't mind being used. By the end of two seasons traveling from rodeo to rodeo, he'd spent more than one night lost in a woman or two. The sex was fun, never serious. And the women were just as happy to see him leave as he was to bid them goodbye.

Harmony, though.

It had always been Harmony.

His own personal ghost.

He tightened his grip on his shaft and closed his eyes. He ran one hand over his tightening balls.

The first time he'd seen her, they were just kids. He was fourteen, fresh from Mexico and still struggling with the language. Her older sister Melody was a senior who'd been assigned as his English tutor. He remembered sitting at the Santos family's kitchen table, learning long lists of vocabulary words, when Harmony would come home from a swim meet dressed in her warm-up suit. She'd make a sandwich for herself and sit down at the same table to do her homework. She was only twelve but so pretty he couldn't take his eyes off her. Like lots of people in the Central Valley, the Santoses were Filipino. Harmony's Asian features came with a complexion the same shade of brown as his own skin.

The more he learned about her, the harder he crushed. She was smart. She was funny. He couldn't always keep up with her lightning-fast English, but when he could, she made him laugh. Years passed. Lucky got a job as a ranch hand with the MacKinnons, close family friends of the Santoses. He saw how protective the MacKinnon brothers were of Melody and Harmony and didn't dare make a move. But God, he wanted to. From afar, he watched Harmony grow up, watched as the boys at school chased her. In his mind, none of them were good enough for her—problem was, he didn't think he was either.

Her skin. *So fucking soft.* He'd run his hands all over her last night and every part of her was soft. Those full, pillowy lips were perfect for kissing. Her hair was cool and heavy. When she wrapped her arms around his bare shoulders, he felt his heart sprint, the beats galloping against his rib cage like hoof beats. When she let him undress her, he almost came in his jeans. For a long time, he didn't get completely undressed for fear that brushing against her would make him ejaculate at once.

Her breasts were big, round, and firm. Her nipples were dark brown with a rosy tinge at the tips. She'd dragged her fingers through his hair as he sucked on her. He'd felt the vibration of her moans through his lips.

And when she opened her legs for him—he'd said a silent prayer to God.

Not the God who'd be pissed off at him for engaging in so much premarital sex. No, not that one. He'd deal with that one later.

But God the creator, who'd made women so endlessly fascinating to him. Lucky was lustful by nature. Women were a special interest of his, and he was always grateful whenever one of them invited him to bed.

But Harmony. God the creator deserved a special prayer of thanks for her.

She wore a lacy thong the color of a ripe peach. He'd primed her body so well that she'd soaked through the fabric, making it even more transparent. She was waxed bare. Lucky would never forget the sight of those dark, wet pussy lips, swollen and plump, barely hidden by that scrap of lace.

In the shower, Lucky speeded up his strokes. His rigid cock thickened. A looming orgasm swirled low in his stomach. He was panting.

He'd hooked her panties with his finger and slid them to the side. The sweet tang of her pussy lingered in his nose and on his tongue. There were few things Lucky enjoyed more than eating a woman out. He was comfortable enough in his masculinity and nothing made him more secure in his machismo than feeling a woman come all over his face. It was better than breaking a pony. And Harmony's pussy tasted like heaven.

She was already on the edge by the time his tongue found her clit. But Harmony knew the score—she held back. When he pushed her, she held back more. She understood. She didn't give up her orgasm without a fight. They flowed like this, back and forth, for a long time. It was a valiant effort, but when he wrested control away from her at last, they both knew who was in charge. She came so hard the first time that she gushed into his mouth, rewarding him with the flavor of her own ecstasy.

Lucky was so turned on, the images and memories started to supersede each other, blending into one. The sensation of impaling her on his cock. The feeling of her gripping him hard as she came a second time. The sight of her heart-shaped ass as he pounded her from behind, playing with her poor little clit until she came again, screaming, her body completely under his charge. When he leaned back, he looked down. In the shadows, her pussy lips gripped his shaft. He was fucking her inside out. Her tiny asshole was slick. His chest tightened when he imagined the things he'd like to do to it.

Fuck.

His balls pulled up against his body. When the orgasm came at last, pleasure drizzled through his nervous system. He opened his eyes and watched the hot come shoot out of his dick onto the tiles. He imagined Harmony on her knees before him, her mouth open to receive it. She'd swallow every drop, then lick her lips like the good girl she was—like the good girl he could make her be in bed.

When he was finished, he cleaned everything up. His heartbeat slowed as turned off the water, toweled off, and got dressed.

The temporary calm that followed climax was quickly replaced with a whole collection of feelings he didn't like. He'd always been an oversexed motherfucker. A mild sense of disgust settled on him along with a litany of doubts and bad feelings.

You just spent the night with the woman of your dreams and you're jacking off again? What the hell is wrong with you?

Another bad feeling.

What were you thinking? Why would you offer to go to a party with her just to make her ex-boyfriend jealous?

Another doubt.

Why are you making things so complicated? Just take this for what it was. A one-night stand you were lucky enough to catch.

And the worst—the absolute worst fear.

You're doing this because you know you're not good enough for her.

He shook off the bad vibes as best as he could.

There were chores to get done before his mother and sister got home for the evening. He prepared *caldo de res* for dinner and pulled up a cabbage and some carrots to add to it. He vacuumed the house. Two loads of laundry, washed, folded, and put away. He saw to his horse and opened up his sister's secondhand laptop to pay some bills online.

Lucky had never been great at school, but numbers he understood pretty well. Everything added up. The household was good for another month. He was obsessed with staying ahead of their bills. Left alone to raise three kids, his mother had struggled for years to make ends meet. Lucky remembered the lights being turned off in his house one night. His younger siblings had cried in the dark as he changed the batteries in the flashlight and sang them Disney songs to calm them down.

After he graduated from high school, instead of applying to community college like his counselors and teachers told him to, he started working full-time at the ranch. He helped Clark sell beef at farmer's markets and made deliveries to restaurants. He and his mom got the bills paid. When his brother was old enough to work after school, they actually were able to save money.

The MacKinnons encouraged Lucky to compete in local rodeos; Dale MacKinnon even paid his first entry fees. He leased horses until Bo Walker cut him that unbelievable price on Batman. And then there was no stopping him—at least until the real world came knocking.

Lucky pulled up the registration and fees for UC Davis, the school his brother Abel attended. He pulled up the pages for the nursing schools his sister wanted to apply to. He scrawled a few numbers on a writing pad and calculated how much he'd have to save to cover their expenses for the next year. In addition to the work he'd pick up where he could, there were three possibilities.

First, he could rob a bank. His mom probably wouldn't be a fan of that.

Second, he could sell Batman. Bo Walker had sold her to Lucky for a song, but Lucky had trained her into one of the best calf-roping horses on the circuit. Everyone knew Batman. With all her tack, her custom saddle, and her trailer, he was certain his horse would fetch a high price. But Lucky's stomach turned when he thought about saying goodbye to her.

Third, he could kick ass in Payson, make it to finals in Las Vegas, and win the world championship buckle as confetti and hundred-dollar bills rained down on him.

Lucky shut the laptop with a soft click and stared at the writing pad. Maybe another answer would show itself. He prayed silently for that answer to come soon.

He stood up and turned off the stove in the kitchen. He locked up the house and started up his truck. He drove to the high school where Araceli was waiting for him after cross-country practice. She climbed into the truck without looking up at him, all of her attention on her phone. He waved a hand in front of her face.

"Hello, zombie."

She swatted his hand away and continued to text. "Cut it out."

Lucky drove down to the motel where his mother sat at the bus stop. She was wearing one of Abel's high school sweatshirts over her work uniform. As always, her hair and makeup were perfect. Lucky pulled over and Araceli slid over as their mother climbed into the cab. She kissed them both on the cheek and clipped on her seatbelt. Lucky caught a slight hint of her perfume, Giorgio Beverly Hills. She'd worn it his entire life.

At home, his mother made a batch of fresh tortillas. They all sat at the table, said a prayer, and ate the soup he'd made with vegetables from their garden and beef from the ranch. After she cleared the table, Araceli started on her precalculus homework. Lucky helped her as much as he could. As always, his mother fell asleep in her chair, watching the evening news.

Lucky stood on the porch after his sister went to bed. In the cold night air, he listened to the deep quiet of the country around him, this place that had somehow become home. He ate another plum and remembered what it was like to sit under the tree with Harmony that afternoon.

How easy it would be to fall in love with her—as easy as taking another sweet bite. The juice ran down his chin, and he wiped it away with his hand.

Lucky remembered digging the hole for that tree and watching his dad plant the sapling. They put the heavy rootball in place, shoveled the dirt back in, and ran a hose to it to soak the soil.

Lucky's dad was tall and handsome, a mythic figure. But Lucky had grown to hate him. He hated that his father had planted them here and left them to fend for themselves. Lucky promised himself a long time ago he would never abandon the people who relied on him. They would never feel vulnerable. They would never sit in the dark afraid. He'd rather die than know he'd let them down.

With that thought fresh in his mind, he pulled his phone out of his pocket and sent a text to Harmony.

Hey. My sister is off this Thursday. Are you working?

A few seconds passed before Harmony's response came. *Yes. I work 8 to 6. Can she be at my apartment at 7:30? Is that too early?*

No. I'll tell her. Lucky smiled to himself. *What about that party? Have you decided?*

Almost two minutes passed before Harmony replied. He imagined her pacing her apartment, weighing her options, and wondering if he truly was as crazy as she thought he was. He imagined her wearing little shorts and a tank top with no bra. He imagined picking her up over his shoulder, tying her up in her own bed, and playing with her beautiful body all night.

The alert on his phone startled him out of his trance. He looked down. *Saturday night. Meet me here at 8?*

Lucky couldn't wait to meet Dr. Dickhead. Much more than that, he couldn't wait to see her again. *Sounds good.* He quickly typed out another text. *So what are you wearing right now?*

The reply came immediately. *Omg, stop.*

What color are your panties?

No response. He typed. *Send me a nude pic?* Winky face.

How about no?

He pictured her rolling her eyes. He laughed quietly. *Okay. Just tits then.*

Good night, Lucky.

A warm feeling descended over him in the quiet. *Good night, belleza.*

What does that mean?

Beautiful.

—◇—

LUCKY GOT a temporary job in the stockroom of the feed-and-tack store in town. Last season, Orbach, the storeowner, had flat-out ignored his requests for sponsorship. Lucky wasn't bitter about it—times were hard everywhere. But when he saw how sloppy and inefficient Orbach was in running his own business, Lucky had a hard time hiding his annoyance. Just a few adjustments here and there would make a big difference in the kind of profits Orbach could make. Lucky had tried to make recommendations, but Orbach made it very clear he'd hired Lucky to push a broom and stock shelves. So Lucky shrugged it off and punched the clock like the robot Orbach assumed he was.

On Tuesdays, Lucky signed on at the sale barn. It was an easy job, loading and working stock while the auction droned on and on.

He brought Batman over to the local rodeo arena. In the evenings, with the stadium lights on, Dean helped him put Batman through her paces. He roped dozens of calves as Dean filmed him. They studied the recordings, taking notes on his form and technique. He worked himself hard, doing runs late into the evening and sleeping like the dead at night only to get up early in the morning to work out and repeat the process again.

On Wednesday night, he nagged his sister to go to bed early. When she wouldn't listen, he took her phone and laptop away and set an old-fashioned alarm clock on her nightstand. "Harmony is doing us a favor. The least you can do is show up on time, ready to learn something."

"Why do you treat me like I'm a little kid? I'm not stupid."

"No, but you don't know your limits, *chamaca*. I know you. You'll be up until one. You need to be on the road by five if you're going to make it on time. You'll be so sleepy everyone at the hospital is going to think you're an idiot. Or worse, you'll crash the truck. Is that what you want?"

She frowned at him. "No."

"Okay, then." He pushed her back on the bed and tucked the covers around her. He couldn't believe his baby sister was already seventeen. Soon she'd be out of the house too. Starting her life, just like their brother. Lucky turned off the light. "Sleep."

"You suck."

"I know." He closed the door. "Good night."

When Araceli got home on Thursday night, it was nearly ten. She came in and quietly walked past their mother asleep in her chair. She made herself a cup of hot chocolate and sat at the table with Lucky as he struggled to stay awake after a long workday.

"How did it go?" he asked.

For the first time in a long time, his sister's eyes were bright and happy. Her phone sat neglected on the kitchen table while she went on and on about what Harmony did and what she'd seen at the hospital.

"And they let me stand behind glass and observe a surgical procedure. This guy had a huge cyst in his armpit and they drained it. It was an ocean of pus!"

Lucky made a face. "Gross."

"No, no, it was so cool, Lucky." As Araceli told him everything, Lucky thought about how good it felt to hear his sister talk about something that interested her. As she'd gotten older, she'd withdrawn from both him and their mother, living a life that was increasingly private and worrisome. Tonight, she was letting him in. And to his relief, the picture of what made her happy was brighter than he'd thought.

She put her mug in the sink. "And Harmony—she's really, really neat. She told me to send her my report card next semester and she'll try to get me a summer internship at the hospital."

"Really?"

"Really." His sister leaned down and gave him a big hug. "Thank you for introducing me to her. And thanks for setting this up."

Lucky squeezed her back. She smelled like a hospital—disinfectant and coffee. "You're welcome, *chamaca*. I'm glad."

—⌖—

WHAT WAS one supposed to wear to a fancy retirement party? Was this going to be one of those wine-and-cheese shindigs where he never had anything to say? Lucky shuddered as he ironed a button-down shirt and starched his good jeans. He brushed his hat and polished his boots. He showered. He was cleaning up his beard with a razor as his sister banged on the door of the bathroom.

"Are you done yet?" she shouted.

"Is it number one? Go do it outside."

"Lucky!"

"God, you and Mom take five years in here and I'm not allowed to complain. I need fifteen minutes and you're about to axe the door like *The Shining*."

"Lu-ckyyyyy!"

Back in his bedroom, he got dressed and put on one of his rodeo buckles. He was adjusting his collar in the mirror when Araceli walked by again. "Where are you going all pretty?" she asked.

"None of your business."

"Ooooh, are you going on a *date*?" She sat down on his bed. "With a *lady*?"

"Go away."

Araceli picked up his phone and unlocked it.

"Hey!" He lunged for it, but she pulled it out of his reach. "How do you know my security code?" He made another grab for it.

Araceli jumped up. *Damn track star.* "You're a cowboy. It's 5150, like that Dierks Bentley song. So predictable."

"What the hell do you know about cowboys?" He cornered her.

She scrolled through his texts. "Oh my God. You're filthy, Lucky. *Cochino.*" Then she looked up at him with an expression of glee. "Yes! I knew it! I knew there was something going on between you two!"

He pinned her against the wall as she squealed like a stuck pig. "Give it back!"

Laughing, Araceli screamed, *"¡Amá, me está golpeando!"*

Their mother walked into the bedroom. *"¿Ahora que pasa?"*

Lucky wrested the phone out of his little sister's talons. As soon as their mother came in, they both switched to Spanish. "I'm not hurting her." He straightened his shirt. "She's being a pain."

Araceli collapsed in a fit of giggles on the bed. She turned to their mother. "Lucky has a big date tonight. With Harmony Santos."

"Harmony Santos? Who's that?"

Lucky's eyes shot daggers at his little sister. "She's just a friend."

"Doesn't he look nice tonight, *Mamá*?" Araceli said. "Harmony's a nurse. She was the one who gave me that tour at the hospital this Thursday. She's really pretty. And really cool."

"A nurse?" His mother raised her eyebrows. "That's nice. Santos. What part of Mexico is her family from?"

Lucky groaned inwardly as he put on his hat. *Here we go.* "She's not Mexican."

"She's not?"

"No. She's Filipino, *Mamá*."

"Filipino?" His mother looked confused for a moment. The thought that her children might date outside their race couldn't have been that strange to her, considering they lived in the Central Valley where everyone was from somewhere else. But he never talked about the women he dated. He didn't know what kinds of assumptions his mother made about his love life.

"A nurse?" his mother said again.

He nodded. "Yes. A nurse."

"Filipino?"

"Yes. Her family's from the Philippines."

His mother paused again. Her carefully painted lips pressed into a worried line. "But she's Catholic, right?"

Lucky cracked a smile. "Yes, she's Catholic." He grabbed his sport coat hanging by the door. "Listen, I have to go or I'll be late."

"Be a good boy, Lucky." His sister wagged her finger at him. "Don't do anything I wouldn't do."

Suppressing a groan, Lucky left the house as quickly as he could. He changed the security code on his phone as soon as he shut the door of his truck.

—❦—

HARMONY LIVED IN A NEW, sterile apartment building made up of two hundred identical units. She buzzed him in, and he took the elevator to the fourth floor. Feeling far more nervous than he expected, he took off his hat and knocked on her door.

When she opened it, Lucky's throat dropped into his stomach and then one more level down into his balls. No doubt about it— the woman was smoking hot. Silky black hair. Cherry-red lips. A purple dress so tight and strappy, his inner kink stood up and said hello. She was barefoot and her toenails were painted red to match her lips. Lucky stood there dumbfounded, his eyes unsure where to linger, indecisive when confronted with so many wonders.

"Hi." Her voice was deeper than most women's. A little whiskey, a little smoke. Hoarse around the edges, as if she'd been screaming his name. Which she had been, a few days ago.

"Hey." He bent down and kissed her cheek. She smelled like orange blossoms.

"I just need to put my shoes on and we can go. Come in for a sec."

Lucky walked into her little apartment. She'd lived there for two years, but the space was as sterile as the rest of the building. Beige couch, a cream-colored rug, a coffee table with a remote control on it. There was no art on the walls, but there was a TV and some kind of gaming system that looked like it cost more than his truck and his horse put together. The entire place was as clean as a hospital, which seemed appropriate considering her profession.

She sat down on the sofa and put on a pair of high-heeled sandals. Her feet were so pretty. He imagined pressing her soles against his chest as he reamed her.

Easy, you pervert.

He cleared his throat. "So where is this party?"

"About a ten-minute drive. Annette has a beautiful house. She restored it. A real Southern belle—from Louisiana. Have you been there?"

He nodded, trying not to stare at her cleavage as she did up the tiny buckles of her shoes. "Couple times. Lafayette."

She admired her toes for a moment then looked up at him. "You've been so many places."

"I only stay long enough for the show. I know more about the highways than I do about the stops."

"Still, I think that's so cool." She stood up and checked her lipstick in the mirror by her front door. "I would love to travel."

She grabbed her purse and keys and put on a leather jacket. She looked so badass that Lucky's palms twitched, aching to strip her bare and spank that sweet ass before he rode it straight to heaven.

"Are you all right?"

He blinked at her. "Huh? Oh, yeah. I'm fine." He put his hat back on and surreptitiously adjusted himself in his jeans. "So, how should we play this?"

"What do you mean?"

"Your ex-boyfriend. How do we make him jealous?"

She looked confused for a moment, as if she'd forgotten the whole purpose of tonight. The expression on her face made Lucky wish he hadn't brought up Dr. Dickhead at all. He cleared his throat. "For example, option one. I could be your dream date. I could pull out your chair for you at the table, get you a glass of wine, laugh at your jokes."

"And option two?

"Option two, I could be a possessive jerk. Hang my arm around you all night. Feel you up and pretend I didn't see him watching."

She smirked. "Why do I get the sense you could play both roles equally well?"

"Actually, I play option two a little better." Lucky's heart skipped at beat when her smirk turned into a genuine smile. "Okay, on a scale of one to ten," he said, "how jealous do you want him to be?"

Instead of answering, Harmony rested her hands on the lapels of his jacket and slid her palms down over his chest. Her eyes rested on his lips. For a moment, Lucky thought she was going to kiss him. His body stilled in anticipation.

"To tell you the truth, I don't know if making Frank jealous is what I really want," she said.

Lucky's heart punched at his ribcage, but he forced himself to stand still. "What do you really want?"

Her soft breaths quickened. Her neck and chest grew flushed. She wanted to kiss him—he could feel it.

"Tell me. What is it you really want?" he asked again.

Harmony looked up into his eyes. "Let's not make a plan," she said slowly. "Let's go to this party and enjoy ourselves. If Frank wants to talk to me, I'll talk to him. If he doesn't, I won't. Whatever happens, happens. Okay?"

Dazed by her, Lucky nodded. "If that's what you want."

"Yes. That's what I want." She patted his chest and dropped her hands. "Let's go." When she turned, he followed her out the door, still starving for that kiss.

They drove a short distance to a large, two-story house in an older part of town. Cars were parked up and down the street. The front of the house was lit up with floodlights. Lucky took her hand as they made their way up the concrete walkway.

"You look so beautiful tonight," he said as they climbed the steps.

"Stop."

"No. I won't. Don't you know how beautiful you are, Harmony? *Hermosa. Preciosa.*"

She smiled shyly at him. "You're not so bad yourself, cowboy." A little dimple formed in her left cheek. He wanted to lick it. He wanted to taste her. No—he *needed* to taste her.

"Wait." Right before she rang the doorbell, he leaned down and kissed those cherry red lips. He whispered, "You know, we don't have to go in. We can just...get back in your car...drive back to your place...and have our own party." He dropped tiny kisses along her jaw. Desire roared in his chest when her breath hitched in her throat. Her cheeks flushed pink. She paused, staring at him as though she were a heartbeat away from taking his suggestion.

Lucky held her gaze. "I've been thinking about you all week." He brushed his fingertips back and forth across the cool, silken skin of her throat. "How about you? Have you been thinking about how good it was?" He lowered his lips to her ear. "Don't you want to play together again?"

Her eyes fluttered closed. "Lucky," she murmured.

"You do, don't you, *belleza*?" He rested his thumb lightly in the hollow of her throat. "Tell me the truth. You've been thinking about me, haven't you?"

The pulse in her neck tapped wildly against his fingers. "Yes, but—"

"Come on," he whispered. "Let's go."

Just then, the front door opened. A glamorous middle-aged woman in a feathered headdress, a masquerade mask, and a green satin dress held out her arms. "There you are! I thought I heard someone out here! I'm so glad you came!" She enveloped Harmony in a big hug. She turned to Lucky and her eyes bugged out of her head. "Oh, my word. Who's this hunky cowboy?" She spoke with an easy Southern accent.

Harmony, a little shaken, cleared her throat. "Annette, this is Lucky Garcia. He's a friend. Lucky, this is Annette Leblanc. She's an administrator at the hospital—I mean, *was* an administrator. This is her retirement party."

To Lucky's surprise, Annette pulled him into another big hug, crushing her ample breasts against his chest. She gave no indication of getting stabbed by his boner. She gave him a loud smacking kiss on the cheek and grabbed their hands. "Lucky, Harmony, welcome, welcome. Come inside and meet everyone."

The house was as beautiful as a museum. About three-dozen people in masquerade masks were milling around and chatting, drinking cocktails out of clear plastic cups served up by a bartender in the corner. A DJ was set up next to the bartender playing brass band music.

Annette took Harmony's jacket and purse. Lucky started to take off his hat, but Annette stopped him. "Oh, no. Keep that on, sweetheart. In fact, add this."

She handed both of them velvet masquerade masks. His was plain black and Harmony's was studded with multicolored sequins. They slipped them on and smiled at each other like dorks.

"Kind of kinky," he said under his breath.

"When in Rome," Harmony said.

Their hostess clapped her hands together with glee. "Oh, Harmony. You look gorgeous. And you, Lucky. You look like the Lone Ranger. Everyone's going to get a *kick* out of you." She threaded her arm through his and pulled him into the room. "Everyone! Look who's here!"

Annette held court. She introduced them to her neighbors and friends, but the guests were mostly hospital staff who greeted Harmony right away. It was hard to read everyone's expressions since their faces were obscured by masks.

Distracted by some issue in the kitchen, Annette released them at last. Lucky found himself growing fond of the hostess— she was full of life, happy to have a beautiful house and beautiful friends to fill it with.

Harmony slipped her little hand into his. The gesture surprised him, particularly in front of all of her coworkers. "Would you like a drink?" she asked.

"Sure," he said.

They went to the bar. "What is everyone drinking?" Harmony asked.

The mustachioed bartender looked back and forth between them. "Hurricanes. Do you want one?"

The music pumped in their ears. Harmony danced to the brassy jazz as they watched the bartender mix up something dangerous with three different bottles of rum and a squirt of pink syrup.

Lucky put a five-spot in the tip jar and took a sip. He made a face. "We're going to get kidnapped by pirates tonight if we drink these."

She put the bright red straw in her lips and took a long drink. "Sounds like fun."

Harmony was popular and beloved among her coworkers, which didn't surprise Lucky at all. They were all happy to see her, and deeply interested in who he was, which did surprise him. She put away her cocktail pretty quickly and soon was laughing and bouncing and bubbly. He'd hidden his drink behind a few picture frames in an attempt to look after his little hurricane, who was perfectly happy to begin an impromptu limbo game with Annette's grandfather's walking stick that someone had found in a hallway closet.

Lucky sat on one of the couches watching Harmony. She drew people to her like a magnet. His skin prickled with mild jealousy when other men at the party talked to her. He wondered which one of these men in masks was her ex-boyfriend. Who was it? Harmony didn't give him any signs.

And then Lucky spotted him. Another guy, hiding in the shadows on the other side of the room. Dressed in an expensive suit and tie. Tall and blond. He was wearing a black mask too, but he'd slid it up. He was staring at Harmony, his features stony and full of melancholy.

Bingo.

Dr. Dickhead.

Had Harmony seen him? Was she ignoring him? Unsure, Lucky watched the motherfucker for five minutes as the game of limbo progressed. Annette had her staff move furniture out of the way as the party guests got more rambunctious. Harmony was their instigator, Peter Pan and Tinkerbell rolled into one. Paying no attention to either Lucky or her ex, Harmony laughed and clapped her hands and snapped endless pictures on her phone.

He wasn't sure what came over him. Lucky got up from his seat on the couch and walked over to where Harmony sat perched on an ottoman, her legs folded beneath her. When he touched her bare shoulder, she looked up in surprise, dark eyes glittering behind her mask.

"Lucky! There you are!" she exclaimed.

He grabbed her arms and hauled her up against his body. His heart was beating hard, and he was having trouble drawing breath. "I have to do this," he whispered.

"Do what?"

He kissed her right there, in the middle of the huge crowd, a dirty openmouthed kiss that couldn't mean anything but *she's mine.* Harmony stared at him, confused, but as he stroked her tongue with his, her eyes went heavy-lidded and her body went slack in his arms. He felt a moan vibrate in her throat, and she kissed him back, gripping his forearms in her hands. She tasted like cherries and dark rum, like all the sweet, wild nights they'd share if only fortune were on his side.

The people at the party began to hoot and cheer, but they meant nothing as far as Lucky was concerned. He was half a breath from dragging Harmony off into a dark corner and screwing her senseless —in the middle of a crowd of strangers, in a house that looked like a museum, while the DJ played Chubby Checker's "Limbo Rock."

So Lucky was justifiably unprepared when a hand yanked his collar backwards and a fist connected with his chin.

Before he knew it, he was flat on his back on the wooden floor, blinking up at the tall blond man with murder in his eyes. "Get up, asshole."

"Frank!" Harmony was yanking on the man's suit jacket. "Frank, stop it!"

Lucky shook off his dizziness and rubbed his sore jaw. The fucker had knocked his hat off his head. That was a death wish in Oleander. Quickly, Lucky sized the guy up. He had an inch or two on Lucky in height, but Lucky had twenty pounds of muscle on him. And no one was faster than a tie-down roper.

Lucky was on his feet in a flash. He rushed Dr. Dickhead, knocking him clear of Harmony. They crashed to the floor, where the good doctor found himself pinned down by two hundred and twenty-five pounds of angry Mexican cowboy. Satisfied to hear the thump of the other man's skull against the parquet, Lucky pounded his face with a series of head shots that would ruin picture day for sure. When Dr. Dickhead looked sufficiently dazed, Lucky backhanded him for good measure. Blood and adrenaline pounded in his veins. It had been a long time since he'd been in a brawl. This one wasn't that great, but the guy had snuck in one good cowardly punch, and Lucky couldn't let him get away with that.

When he stood up, Lucky was breathing hard and his muscles twitched, flooded with adrenaline. He forced himself to calm down. He knew this feeling well—it was the same feeling he had in the rodeo arena after a good run.

He picked up his hat and took off the mask. It was then that he realized the music had stopped. He looked around. Everyone in the party was staring at him. Some of them had taken off their masks too. Their faces registered fear. Disgust. Embarrassment. Shame.

What's happening? Why is everyone looking at me like that? He searched the room. *Where's Harmony?*

Annette came out of the crowd and ushered him to the door, all mirth gone. "You need to go now."

"What? What have I done?" he asked. "He hit me first."

"I know, sweetheart. But that was…that was brutal."

Brutal?

Lucky and his friends beat the shit out of each other on a regular basis. Surely these people didn't think he was some kind of deviant because he knew how to fight. He took another deep breath and put his hat back on. "I'm sorry, Annette. I didn't mean to ruin your party. Where is Harmony? I'll take her home now."

The loquacious woman said nothing, but the expression on Annette's face would stay with Lucky for a long time. Wide-eyed. Ashen.

She's afraid of me. She thinks I'll hurt Harmony.

He glanced past Annette's shoulder. Harmony, in her purple dress, was leaning over Frank, trying to revive him. Someone handed her a wet towel. She took it and pressed it to the doctor's face. Tears were rolling down her cheeks.

And Lucky knew.

He didn't mean anything to Harmony. Just like she'd said, he was a distraction—nothing more. The man she loved was here, but he wasn't it.

He looked at Annette and nodded. "All right. Please, just look after her for me."

"I will, sweetheart."

Lucky left the house. As he walked the few miles back to Harmony's apartment, cold seeped into his damp clothes and chilled him. With each step, his jaw began to throb. It would be swollen tomorrow, making him look like the monster he felt like inside.

You were right. You're not good enough for her. Her world isn't yours.

AFTER A FEW DAYS, the swelling in Lucky's jaw went down at last. Seeing what a dark mood her brother was in, Araceli didn't tease him about Harmony. Both his sister and his mother knew things had gone horribly wrong on his date, and if he wanted to tell them more, he would open up in his own time. For now, they steered clear, giving him lots of space.

He worked at the feed and tack store. He put in his hours at the sale barn. Every night, he worked with Batman until he was so sore he couldn't lift his arm.

On Wednesday, at the rodeo arena, Dean and Lucky watched the video of his last run. For some reason, Batman had been slow in sliding to a stop as soon as the calf was roped around the neck. Lucky racked his brains to figure out why. Dean made a few suggestions that seemed to work, but Lucky's times had not improved in the last two weeks. He'd be leaving for Arizona in a couple days.

"You've been working yourself too hard. How's the shoulder?" Dean asked.

"I've been icing it down at night."

"Take it easy. You're going to hurt yourself before Payson."

Dean was right. "I know," Lucky said.

"And the knee?"

Lucky had twisted his knee late last season and had to undergo weeks of physical therapy for it. It was the reason he was out of the running for world finals last year. "It's okay. I don't feel it much anymore."

Dean nodded and searched his face. The eldest MacKinnon brother had always been an intimidating figure to Lucky. As a professional bullfighter, Dean had stared down eighteen-hundred-pound bulls in the arena, protecting bull riders who'd been bucked off. He'd retired from the professional arena last year. He continued to work cattle on the ranch and ran a bull-fighting and bull riding school with Bo Walker, the stock contractor in nearby Lake Isabella.

So Dean would understand Lucky's particular conundrum more than anyone else.

"Do you miss it?" Lucky asked. "Do you miss being on the road? All those shows?"

Dean shrugged. "From time to time. I miss the excitement. But I sure as hell don't miss being away from home." Since he'd gotten married and had a son, Dean was as steady as an oak tree, as hard a worker as his father had been. "Truth is, I don't have much time to miss it. I don't have time for much of anything these days."

"I know how busy you are. Thanks for helping me out with all of this."

"Don't sweat it. This is how I unwind. I get to take a little break from changing diapers and washing milk bottles." Dean closed the laptop. "Tell me the truth. Are you still thinking of giving this up? Selling your horse?"

"Araceli's starting college next year. With her and Abel enrolled at the same time, I don't know how we'll swing it. I need to find steady work—these odd jobs, they're not enough. And we can't rely on my winnings—too unpredictable."

Dean rubbed his beard. "Steady work, huh? I might have a lead for you. Give me a few days to find out more."

"I'd appreciate it. Anything. You know I'm down for it."

"I gotta be honest, Luck. You giving this up—it tans my hide. Ranch or rodeo, you're one of the best cowboys I've ever met. You've got a gift."

"It's not really a gift. No one gave it to me. I had to work my ass off for it." Lucky stood up and stretched out his shoulder.

"What else is bothering you? This whole week you've been distracted. What's up?"

Nothing escaped Dean. His sixth sense for reading livestock carried over to people. Lucky leaned up against the rails. Time to confess. "It's Harmony."

"Harmony?"

"It's…complicated."

"Of course it's complicated." Dean smiled to himself. "Lay it on me, Luck."

Except for the part where he banged Harmony to three screaming orgasms in the bunkhouse, Lucky told Dean everything. From the opening of the Silver Spur to the final moment on the doorstep of Annette Leblanc's house. He'd been torn up, inside out, for days. Only his own shame kept him from calling her. She'd texted him a couple times. He didn't respond. Not to be a dick, but to keep distance between them. She obviously loved Frank. Why would Lucky complicate that with something as inconsequential as a childhood crush? Who was he fooling? She wasn't part of his world. She was destined to love a Lockwood, not a Garcia.

Dean kicked back in his folding chair and listened in silence. When Lucky was done, he shook his head slowly. "Jesus. That is some shit."

"Some shit," Lucky agreed.

"What are you going to do?"

"What am I going to do? Nothing. You should've seen her. Leaning over him. Wiping his face. Crying. Fuck, if a woman felt like that about me after I got my ass kicked, I'd have it made. I won that fight and what did I get? They all looked at me like I was some kind of monster." Lucky paused, shame clawing at his insides. "I never want to be looked at like that again."

"Don't worry about them. They're just not used to our brand of diplomacy."

"What should I do? Do you think I should call her?"

"Yeah. Call her. Talk it out. What you feel is what you feel. You have no way of knowing the truth until she tells you." Dean nodded thoughtfully. "You may be right about her not wanting to have anything to do with you. But I watched that girl grow up. It would take a lot more than a brawl to scare Harmony Santos off. Trust me."

—❦—

THE NEXT MORNING, Lucky texted her. She didn't text him back. He called her. She didn't pick up.

Serves you right for not answering her calls first. What was the saying? Karma's a bitch.

When her voicemail beeped, he cleared his throat. "Harmony. This is Lucky. I just wanted to…to talk to you and see how you are. I know it's been a few days. I'm sorry I didn't answer your texts earlier. I guess I needed to simmer down a little bit." He paused. "I didn't know what to say. I guess." He groaned inwardly at his awkwardness. "Anyhow, please call me. I want to tell you something important. Okay. Bye."

She didn't respond all day. Before he could second-guess himself, he got in his truck after work and drove to Bakersfield to see her. He parked outside her apartment building to pump himself up. Fog had gathered in the valley. The street lamps shimmered through the thick vapor, creating ghosts of light on the wet asphalt.

He rubbed his hands together and summoned up his courage.

With a dreamy sigh, he thought about her sitting under the plum tree with him. Sunlight, glittering through the leaves, illuminating her cheeks. Her lips, wet with sweet juice.

Lockwood was a doctor from the wealthiest family in the county. How could he compete with that? What did he have to offer her?

A rickety bench. A handful of fruit. A patch of dirt. A horse. His beat-up body. The anger of an abandoned son. The forever-looming shadow of debt, almost too fast for him to outrun. He still had nightmares about it, about the lights being turned off. He'd never forget the way his nine-year-old brother cried or the way his seven-year-old sister wailed, holding on to him in the dark.

But what else did he have to offer Harmony?

His brain, for one. He had given up his chance of going to college, but he knew he was smart. He understood numbers better than people who had more education than him. And Dean was right. He was a damned good cowboy—he'd worked cattle all his life, even back in Zacatecas. He rode horses before he could walk.

Most of all, Lucky was sure of one thing. He knew no one *loved* the way he did.

It was hard to articulate this quality. All he knew was if Harmony was his, he'd give his life to see her happy. He'd give her everything he had, inside and out.

But how could he tell her that he had nothing to give her now except everything he was *going* to do? The outline of kingdoms he would build, lands he would conquer for her?

Right now, they were only imaginary kingdoms. Empty spaces on a map.

How did that make him different from his father?

Lucky looked at himself in the rearview mirror. He was *nothing* like his father.

He took one more deep breath and put his hand on the door handle of his truck.

Do it.

Before he opened his door, two figures appeared in the fog. They were walking side by side towards his truck. Talking, they approached the front gate of the apartment and the woman tapped in a code.

Lucky narrowed his eyes. She was dressed in a jacket, jeans, and cowboy boots. She had dark hair. The man was tall and dressed in a suit. He had blond hair. When he stepped into the light from the street lamp, Lucky saw that his face was beat to shit, lip split with a black eye fading to purple.

They laughed at something. The metal gate buzzed open. The man opened the door. Harmony walked in. The doctor followed her inside and the gate slammed shut.

Lucky gripped the steering wheel to keep himself together. He sat frozen, unsure of what to do. All of the courage he'd gathered a minute earlier dissipated like smoke, replaced by a different voice.

Don't confuse fantasy for reality. One night doesn't mean anything.

Shoving his feelings deep down inside, Lucky tapped his fist on the dashboard.

You were a distraction. She told you so.

He turned the key and started up his engine.

This was a mistake. She's not yours. She never was. She never will be.

He put the truck in drive and started back for Oleander.

--⟨⟩--

FRIDAY EVENING at the Silver Spur. Sitting at a table with Clark and Daniel MacKinnon, Lucky worked on his Jack and Coke. It wasn't his first. The floor was crowded with giggly newbies taking line-dancing lessons. Lucky figured that for every replay of "Achy Breaky Heart," Billy Ray Cyrus deserved at least six hours in purgatory.

"So what's this big announcement?" Lucky was already slurring a little.

Daniel shrugged. "Dean said to meet him here at eight. That's all I know."

"Another kid?" Clark asked.

"I don't think so. Too soon, even by our standards." Daniel sipped his beer. "So, when are you planning on starting work on the farmhouse?"

"We're shooting for next month," said Clark. "Copper piping. New roof. And we're going to add that suite for Mom on the first floor. She wants a big south-facing room. Lots of sun."

"Let me know who you're working with. We had some good

guys when we built our house. That was what, twelve years ago? The work's still sound."

"I will. Melody wants to make sure everyone we work with's licensed and bonded."

"I don't blame her. It's an old house. Lots of quirks."

Lucky groaned inwardly. *Wives, babies, houses.* All he wanted was to get drunk. He polished off his cocktail and attempted to wave a server over for another.

"Hey." Clark elbowed him. "You okay?"

"Yeah. I just need a drink."

"Or three?"

"Or four."

Clark narrowed his eyes at Lucky. "Is this about—"

"Don't. I don't want to talk about it."

Clark said nothing more. Daniel held out his hand. "Keys."

True friends. Lucky handed Daniel the keys to his truck. When Lucky shook the ice in his glass, one of the Spur's new cocktail waitresses, a college cutie with pink hair and an upturned nose, sauntered over. "What can I getcha?" She stood close enough for Lucky to smell her perfume. Vanilla, sweet and heady.

"Another Jack and Coke," he said.

"You got it, cowboy."

Lucky was well pickled by the time Dean arrived. He'd driven straight from Walker Ranch in Lake Isabella and ordered a round for all of them before he sat down at the table.

"Suspense is not my thing," said Clark. "Spill it."

Dean cleared his throat. "Bo's retiring. He wants me to take over."

"The ranch? The rough stock?" asked Daniel.

"All of it." The bullfighter grinned. "We've been working on this deal for two months. Our lawyers finalized the paperwork today. Walker Ranch is now Walker-MacKinnon Ranch. And you are looking at its new owner. Dean MacKinnon, bona-fide stock contractor."

"Ho-leeeeee shit," Clark said.

Whoops, hollers, backslaps. Bo Walker had bred bucking bulls and pickup horses for more than three decades. His operation was the envy of stock contractors all over the country. Semen straws from his champion bull Dandelion Wine were almost two grand a pop. Bo and Dean had forged a bond back when Dean was an up-and-coming bullfighter looking for a mentor. They'd been friends ever since.

Lucky raised his glass and the brothers clinked their beer bottles against it. "Congratulations, Dean," he said, and meant it. The MacKinnons were on a roll—but Lucky was not a MacKinnon, last time he checked.

He shot the shit with his friends at the table, riding the ebb and flow of his buzz. When he was feeling a little steadier on his feet, he joined the crowd on the dance floor. He knew all of these dances by heart. Even a few fingers of Jack Daniels couldn't make him forget the steps. "Watermelon Crawl" was followed by Alan Jackson's "Good Time." By the second chorus, Lucky was almost convinced he was having a good time himself. When the flashbacks started, he tried to erase each memory with another dance or another drink.

Harmony petting Batman's nose and laughing as his horse drooled on her? "Boot Scootin' Boogie."

Harmony sitting on the ottoman at Annette Leblanc's party, laughing and barefoot? "Country Girl Shake It For Me."

Harmony holding him tight, shuddering and gasping as she came? Another Jack and Coke.

Harmony asleep on his chest as he stroked her hair? Jack on the rocks, hold the Coke.

Harmony laughing as the doctor followed her upstairs? Jack. Hold the rocks, hold the Coke.

Lucky was lost in a haze of his own bad decisions when he

found himself sitting on a milk crate behind the bar, arms crossed, his head tipped forward as a pair of unknown hands rubbed his shoulders.

"Easy does it."

The hands massaged his neck. Cool thumbs dug into his hot flesh. He groaned.

Someone whispered in his ear. "You are the hottest thing in this shithole, you know that?"

He was barely conscious when a girl appeared in his lap. Surprised, he lost his balance, unfolded his arms and reached out to steady himself against a nearby Dumpster. The girl straddled him and laced her hands tightly around the back of his neck. Before he could react, she covered his mouth with hers. Lucky's eyes shot open. The pink-haired cocktail waitress. She smelled so strongly of vanilla, his stomach turned at the cloying perfume. Lucky jerked his head back as he broke the kiss. "Hey, wait—"

She clung to him. "Shh."

Alarms went off in his head as he struggled to stand up. The milk crate fell over with a crash as he got to his feet. The young woman dragged his head down for another kiss. When he slipped out of her grasp, she reached for his belt buckle. He tried to dodge her again. Whiskey had muddled his reflexes. She caught him, undid his fly, and pushed him against the wall.

He swayed on his feet as he tried to pull the zipper back up. "This is a bad idea."

She pushed his hands away with a wicked smile and undid the top button of his jeans. "I'll make it good for you."

"I don't want this." He stepped sideways out of her grasp. He was going to be sick.

"Trust me, baby. You do."

"No, no—"

"Get off him." In a flash, the waitress was on her back on the asphalt, coughing and sputtering, the wind knocked out of her. Confused, Lucky looked up and saw Harmony, in boots, jeans, and an old T-shirt that said *Hello Nurse*. Her hands were curled into fists and her cheeks were rosy with anger. "Your boss is gonna hear about this, you shady little shit."

The young woman struggled to her feet. Harmony had thrown her hard, judo-style. The girl's watery eyes burned with fury. "Crazy Chinese bitch."

Harmony pointed to herself. "Filipino. Crazy *Filipino* bitch."

Just then, the back door banged open and out walked the MacKinnons, beer bottles in hand. "What'd we miss?" Clark asked, looking from Lucky to Harmony and back.

Outgunned, the furious cocktail waitress limped back into the bar.

Harmony gave Clark a shove. "Why weren't you guys watching Lucky? He's wasted."

"Lucky? I thought he was in the shitter. How you doin', kid?"

Lucky took a deep breath and swayed. "Not so great, Superman." He took two steps towards Harmony, paused, bent over, and dumped a bucketful of hot puke at her feet. As he heaved, Lucky wished the ground would open up and swallow him whole at last. The MacKinnons were laughing up a storm.

Harmony, unmoved by bodily fluids of any kind, shook her head and sighed.

"Help me get him home, you gorillas," she said.

TWO WRAPS AND A HOOEY

"In any case you mustn't confuse a single failure with a final
defeat."
—F. Scott Fitzgerald

When Lucky's alarm went off that morning, the sharp
sound pierced his eye sockets like ice picks. After a long
make-out session with the toilet, he took a hot shower, drank a
cup of coffee, and survived a furious glare from his mother
before he left for work. Like a good robot, he put in his hours at
the feed store. He'd worked through a hangover before but never
like this. By noon, he'd vowed never to touch a drop of Jack
Daniels again. His head throbbed like it had been trampled by
every horse in the state of Tennessee.

At quitting time, Lucky got his jacket on and shuffled out to
the parking lot before Orbach could give him a talking-to. He
needed this job—at least until he gave up rodeo for good. Then
he'd be able to find better work.

With a weary sigh, he sat in his truck and checked his

messages. Harmony had sent him two while he was getting drunk at the Spur. One read, *Phone ran out of battery. Got your messages. Call me.* The other one read, *Where are you? Mel said you're at the Spur. Call me.* There were no other texts from her.

Lucky stared at his phone. This was the worst game of phone tag ever. After the party at Annette Leblanc's, he'd ignored Harmony's texts. When he'd gotten the guts to call her at last, her phone had run out of battery. After what he'd seen at the apartment, she'd texted him again, but he was too drunk to pick up. She'd turned up at the Spur and saved him from a tiny, horny racist. After that? Nothing. Not a peep.

Did she still want to talk to him? He'd embarrassed her at the party, acted like an ass by not answering her calls, and barfed all over her boots.

He groaned.

But she'd left him messages. And she'd done a good thing, looking after him last night. Being her boyfriend was definitely off the table. But being her friend? Maybe he could still be that—if he thanked her and apologized for his douchebag behavior.

Before he lost his nerve, he dialed her number. She picked up on the fourth ring. "Oh, good, you're alive."

"Barely." He rubbed the bridge of his nose. "Do you have a second? Can you talk?"

"Yeah."

"Okay. Two things." He took off his hat and put it on the dashboard. He leaned back and shut his eyes. His head still ached. "First off, thank you for last night. I acted like an idiot. You don't have to believe me, but I don't usually get carried away like that." Lucky thought about the disaster by the Dumpster. "I don't know what would've happened if you hadn't turned up. Nothing good."

"Probably not."

"Also, I wanted to apologize for the party. At Annette's. What I did—that was uncalled for." He didn't truly believe that last part, but it felt like the right thing to say. "I'm sorry. I got carried away. I forgot where I was. I disrespected you and your boyfriend."

"My boyfriend?" She was quiet for a second. "Lucky, tell me something."

"What?"

"Why were you getting shitfaced at the Spur last night?"

Think fast. "Dean. Dean's taking ownership of Walker Ranch. He wanted to celebrate."

"Any reason you were drinking whiskey while the other guys were drinking Bud?"

Yeah. You. "No, not really. Just a case of nerves, I guess. Qualifying for finals and everything." Lucky winced. He didn't like lying to her. Then something occurred to him. "Why were *you* at the Spur last night?"

"Your messages," she said. "I was worried about you."

"About me?"

"I forgot my phone charger at home. I didn't receive your messages until I got back from the hospital. When you didn't text back, I called my sister. She told me where you were." She sighed. "So I came out to see you."

"Why would you do that?"

She paused. "Like I said. I was worried."

"That's a long drive. Didn't Dr. Dickhead mind?"

"What are you talking about?"

"I saw him, Harm. I saw him go upstairs with you. Thursday night, I came out to visit you. To apologize. To talk to you in person. But you were with him. So I left." *Yes, that's it. Perfect. Confess what a creepy loser you are.* "It makes no difference anyway. You love him. It's obvious."

"Obvious, huh?" Her voice was sarcastic. "So what happened between you and me? What was that?"

That caught him off guard. "What we had was a one-night stand. It was good—it was amazing, to tell the truth. But it was a mistake." The word cut him. "This is going to sound really pathetic, but mistake or not, I still feel lucky to have shared it with you. Just so you know."

Silence stretched between them like a bridge that was too weak to cross safely. Then Harmony crossed it. "You're wrong."

"Wrong? How am I wrong?"

"Frank is not my boyfriend. We didn't get back together."

"I know what I saw. No girl cries over a guy who's just gotten his ass beat unless she loves him."

"Or she's drunk and furious. I tried to hold you both back. You both ignored me. Some girls fantasize about two guys fighting over them. Not me. My friends, my coworkers— everyone was there, watching. It was embarrassing. Then when I looked for you afterwards, Annette told me you'd gone home."

Lucky hadn't considered the situation from her perspective. "How about what I saw at your apartment? He went upstairs with you. You were *laughing*."

"I was laughing about what I was going to do with his Play-Station if he hadn't come to pick it up. I told him I was going to sell it and pocket the money." She paused. "That's what he was doing at my place. Picking up his crap. What am I going to do with a brand-new PlayStation? I don't play."

Lucky remembered seeing the system in her living room. "Basically, what you're saying is…you're not together?"

"No. We're not."

"At all?"

She took a deep breath. "We talked it out. Shouted it out, more like. I got to the truth. He's got big plans to leave Bakersfield and travel the world."

"Don't you want to travel too? Don't you want to go with him?"

"I thought I would. But in the time we've spent apart, I finally got the chance to look at our relationship objectively. And I saw things I hadn't seen before."

"Like what?"

"Lots of things." She sighed. "For example, the whole time we were together, I second-guessed myself. I tried to be everything he told me I should be. Less impulsive. Less immature. Less crazy. More like him."

"I never thought you were immature. Crazy, maybe." He paused. "The best kind of crazy."

She sniffed, a little puff of laughter that made Lucky smile. "We had been growing apart for months. I was just too short-sighted to realize it. Frank is capable of a lot of good in his life. But it's hard for him to see beyond his own career. He wants to make decisions for both of us. And that just doesn't work for me."

"So what works for you?"

"Maybe I just need to find someone who appreciates my kind of crazy."

A minute passed as Lucky processed what she'd just said. Absently, he played with the edge of a piece of duct tape he'd used to repair a tear in his upholstery. "Just to be clear, that's it? That's it between you two?"

"That's it."

He suppressed the urge to cheer. "So."

"So."

"Back to this 'you and me' idea."

"What about it?"

"I think we should look into it a little more."

She paused. "Only if you answer a question for me."

"What's that, *belleza*?"

"Why were you getting shitfaced at the Spur last night?"

Lucky groaned. "Really? You're really asking me that?"

"Yes! And it wasn't because of Dean or because of finals. Stop lying to me."

"Jesus Christ." This girl was driving him crazy. She always had. He gathered his courage. "All right. Fine. Here it is. I was drinking because—"

"Yes, I'm listening."

"Do you want me to tell you or not?"

She laughed softly. "Tell me."

"I was drinking because"—his heart beat faster, but his head got clearer—"I didn't like seeing you with your ex. After the night we spent together, I thought I might have a chance with you."

She stopped laughing. "Honest to God?"

"Honest to God. Harmony, do you know how long I've had a crush on you? Do you have any idea?"

She said nothing.

Just when it seems impossible to get any creepier, you manage to do it. Good job, fucker. Lucky cleared his throat. "So, um. Are you with your sister? Or are you in Bakersfield?"

"Bakersfield," she said softly. "When are you leaving for Arizona?"

"Tomorrow."

Harmony was silent for a long time. Lucky waited. When she spoke at last, her voice was rough. "I want to see you. Before you go."

Lucky sat up and shoved his key into the ignition. "I'm on my way."

❧

HARMONY SHOWERED AND SHAVED, slathered herself with lotion, and dried her hair. After putting on a little tinted lip balm and waterproof mascara, she stood in front of her closet. What did one wear for a booty call? What would Lucky like? She settled on nothing and put on her robe.

Harmony turned the air conditioning and tightened the belt on her robe. She listened to something sad on the country radio station as she changed the sheets on her bed. After that, she sat on a chair by the window and looked out at the dark, empty street.

Lucky had been there, just a few days ago. Waiting in his

truck for her to get home. He wasn't a stranger. He wasn't a friend. The logical part of her brain told her she should've been creeped out by him waiting for her at home. But the rest of her brain—as well as her body—felt a jumpy kind of excitement. He'd been thinking about her. Waiting. Wanting.

Now it was her turn to wait.

She closed her eyes and remembered the sight of him above her in the bunkhouse. Even now, days later, her body tightened at the memory.

She wanted him. He'd reached some tender place inside her that Frank had never reached. Vulnerability was something she'd always fought, but somehow, she wanted to be vulnerable for Lucky. She wanted to be naked for him—naked in a way she had never been for any man.

Curious, her nerves tingling, she reached down between her legs. She was slick and swollen. Thinking about her ex-boyfriend had never made her feel like this.

Harmony stared at the street, willing Lucky's truck to appear. The blinds were open, but the windowsill was level with her collarbone. Anyone walking by would see her sitting in her window. She scooted her chair closer to the wall. She began to touch herself. With her fingertips, she rubbed the smooth skin just above her clit. Her whole body grew warm. She took deep, slow breaths that brought fresh blood to her pussy.

God, she wanted him. She'd thought about Lucky the entire drive to the Spur. Anger, possessive and primitive—that's what she'd felt upon seeing another woman all over him. And she'd thought about Lucky the entire drive back to Bakersfield, wishing things had been different.

Seeing him hurting had given her a perverse kind of hope. Maybe he'd been drinking because he wanted her. Maybe he'd been as hungry for her as she had been for him this whole week. And she was right. He'd felt the same way.

She contemplated getting up to fetch the vibrator in her

nightstand. No—she shouldn't be impatient. Lucky would take the orgasm out of her soon enough. Just like he had that night in the bunkhouse. Three big ones, wild and raw. She was thirsty for him. She wanted him bad.

Goddamn—she had never been this horny before. Gingerly, she ran the pad of her middle finger over her slick, hardened clit, playing cat and mouse with her orgasm. She clenched and held back. She stroked herself and held back again. She opened her legs wider.

Where are you, Lucky?

She was in a hot lather when at last his truck appeared on the street. He parked and turned off his engine. He jumped right out and strode to the entrance of her building without hesitation. Harmony's heart was pounding. She went over to the telephone and picked it up as soon as it rang.

"It's me."

"I know." She hit the button and the gate buzzed open.

She counted down in her head. He'd take the elevator to the fourth floor. He'd walk down the hall. He'd find her apartment. Blood pounding in her ears, she stood by the front door, pussy already wet, nipples already hard. In one wild night, he'd turned her into an animal. There was no way she'd think of sex the same way again. There was nice sex. There was pleasant sex. There was even satisfying sex. But sex with Lucky? He'd turned her whole world upside down.

He knocked. Trembling, almost too horny to see straight, she forced herself to stand still for a moment, savoring the anticipation. Thirty seconds passed. She opened the door.

Lucky looked up under the brim of his hat. Staring at him, she untied her robe and held it open. His dark gaze slid down her naked body and back up to her face. If someone had walked by in the hallway, they would've gotten an eyeful. Lucky sure did.

Two big steps and he was inside her apartment. He slammed the door behind him.

"You crazy motherfucker," she whispered.

He said nothing, grabbed her, and pulled her hard against him. His clothes and hands were cool against her bare skin. But when he kissed her, his lips were scorching. She took his face in her hands. Feverish. His mouth tasted like coffee and cinnamon gum. When his tongue found hers, she caught his true flavor, the taste of his body. Salt. Sex.

Locked in a ravenous kiss, he lifted her high off the ground, and she wrapped her legs around his lean hips. On fire, she took off his hat and dropped it on the ground. He bit her bottom lip gently. She moaned. She dug her hands into his thick hair and pulled his head back so that she could kiss his neck, just where the soft hair of his beard ended and his rough, stubbled skin began. As Harmony covered his throat with hungry, open-mouthed kisses, Lucky carried her to the sofa and sat down.

She straddled his steel-hard thighs. He pulled back and looked at her with those hooded eyes. He was breathing hard. Staring down at her naked body, he ran his fingers through her hair and grazed a line from her temple to her jaw with his rough knuckles. Then he did something that no man had ever done to her. He rested his big hand on her neck. He didn't grab or choke her, but the sensation of his palm and fingers on her throat made Harmony's heart beat madly. Her pussy grew even wetter.

He noticed her reaction and looked her in the eye. "Do you like this?"

Mesmerized, Harmony gasped and grabbed his forearm. "Yes."

How did he do this to her? He'd been in her apartment for two minutes and already he'd taught her something new about her body. He leaned forward and kissed her so softly, she turned to liquid in his grip. "Have you played rough before?"

"Not really," she whispered. His forearm was solid muscle in her hands. "Only with you."

He grinned. "You mean the other night? I wasn't rough with you. But"—he kissed her lips again—"I can be. Tonight. If that's what you want." His eyes glittered. "Is that what you want, Harmony?"

Her pulse beat wildly against his fingers. "Yes."

Still holding her neck, he kissed her cheek. "All right. Listen carefully," he whispered in her ear. "'Yellow.' That means slow down. I'll check in with you to see if you're okay. 'Red' means stop. I'll stop right away. Understand?"

"Yes." She paused. "Is there a word for 'more'?"

"Just say 'more.' If you can't talk but you want to say something, grunt twice and I'll take out the gag—whatever it is." He smiled. "Okay?"

"Okay."

His fingers massaged her neck gently but firmly. "Is there anything you don't want me to do to you?"

She closed her eyes, trying to concentrate. She thought of porn she'd seen. Erotic novels she'd read. "I don't...I don't want you to bite me. Or spit on me." This was surreal. Was this really happening to her? Or was this some kind of fever dream? She opened her eyes. "How about you?"

"My words are the same," he said, "but I don't think there's anything I wouldn't let you do to me." He kissed her yet again. "Last question. On a scale of one to ten, how rough do you want me to be with you tonight?"

She blinked. No one had ever been rough with her, so she had no context. Playing it safe, she whispered, "Seven."

One more kiss. "Lucky number seven it is."

He lifted her off his lap and sat her on the sofa. He stood up. She watched as he undressed for her, piece by piece. Jacket, T-shirt, boots, socks, belt, jeans. When he took off his boxer briefs, his raging erection bobbed free. Finally, she got a good look at him—his dusky cock was long and mouthwateringly thick. Her pussy clenched with hunger.

"Get on your knees." His voice was flinty.

She knelt before him on the carpet and looked up. Past the

breathtaking abs and rock-hard chest was a face made for fantasy: deep-browed, dark-eyed, sensual. He wasn't smiling. "Suck my dick."

Turned on beyond belief, Harmony slid forward. She took his shaft in both hands. It was like grabbing the handle of a hot pan. Heat radiated from him. She gripped the base. Gazing upward, wanting to please him, she circled the head of his cock with the tip of her tongue.

His face remained still while his chest rose and fell rapidly. "I didn't say tease me, Harmony." He didn't raise his voice, but she could feel the steel in it. "I said suck. My. Dick."

She pressed her lips together, wetting them until they were slick. He was already hard as a baseball bat. With a deep breath, she opened wide and slid him deep inside. Savoring his rich, clean taste, she concentrated on shaping her mouth around him. As she began her first strokes, she made sure to grip him with the softest part of her lips, just inside. As she grasped his shaft in her fist, she reached up and cradled his balls in her cupped hand.

Lucky hissed between his teeth. He ran his fingers through her hair and grasped it gently by the roots. "Like that." He gazed down at her as she looked up at him, seeking approval. "Yes. Just like that, *belleza.*"

She watched his face as she sucked him off, reading each reaction, learning what turned him on. His breath quickened when she ran her tongue along the notch on the underside of his cock where the head met the shaft. He flexed his thighs on the downstroke, and he groaned when she took him deep while licking the hard tendon at the base of his cock.

Taking her time, she rested her hands on his lean hips and grazed his skin with her fingernails. Her lips were wet. Then her chin. Then her throat. Minutes passed. She closed her eyes and lost herself, surrendering to the exquisite satisfaction of pleasing him the way he'd pleased her.

She speeded up her strokes and opened her eyes again. His

abs were flexed tight, and his body was glistening with sweat. He put his hand under her chin and whispered. "Enough."

Panting, Harmony slid backwards off his cock. He grabbed her arms and pulled her up. Eyes aflame, he kissed her swollen lips, wrapped his arms around her hips and lifted her again. They kissed as he carried her down her own hallway to her bedroom. Holding her with one enormous arm, he opened the door and flipped on the lights.

He broke their kiss. "I don't want it dark. I want to see every inch of you when we do this."

Harmony's heart was beating so hard she thought it would burst out of her chest. He set her down on the floor and slipped the silk robe from her shoulders. Eyes burning into hers, he pulled the belt out of its loops and pointed to the bed behind her. "Lie down."

The quilt on her bed was ice cold against her feverish skin. Suddenly, Lucky was above her. His big, rough hands clapped around her wrists as he yanked her arms over her head. In a heartbeat, he'd tied both her hands together and lashed them to her headboard.

He looked down at her. "Try to get out."

Smiling, she squirmed and tried to wiggle out. Nothing.

"Didn't think so." He smirked and plucked the taut belt like a guitar string. With a searing kiss, he ran his hands up and down the sides of her body. Then he stopped and stood up.

Harmony's eyes shot open at the abrupt separation. "Wh-where are you going?"

"Exploring."

"Exploring?"

Lucky opened her closet and rifled through her clothes. The hangers scraped quietly on the bar. "So many sexy dresses. Can't wait to see you in them."

"Lucky! Cut it out."

"Cut what out?"

"Being nosy." She yanked on the belt.

He ignored her and looked down at the shoeboxes stacked on the floor of her closet. He whistled low. "That's a lot of shoes for only two little feet."

"Make an Imelda Marcos joke and I'll knee you in the balls."

He smiled and looked at the back of her closet where she'd stashed all her posters. "What's all that?"

"What?"

"These frames." He pulled one out. Van Gogh's *Irises*. Her sister had bought it for her in Los Angeles. There were five or six framed posters in the closet. "Why are all these hidden in here?"

Harmony twisted in her restraints, impatient. "I took them down."

"Why?"

"Dumb reasons."

"Like what?"

She sighed. "My ex said I had generic taste in art. He was going to bring me better art to put up. He never did, though."

"Generic?" Lucky looked over the art with a thoughtful expression on his face. "Do you like it?" He held it up for her to see.

The expressive lines. The grayish-greens. The one white blossom lost among the blues. "Of course I do," she said quietly. "I think it's pretty. And Mel bought it for me."

"So why'd you take it down?"

"Come on, Lucky."

He raised his eyebrows. "Answer the question."

"I don't know." She sighed. "I guess I just wanted to be more… sophisticated. Frank knew so much more about things than I did."

"Did he? Really?" Lucky looked around her bedroom. There was a hook on the wall. Carefully, he hung the painting back up. "But he didn't know what you liked." He looked at the picture and straightened it. "There. Better, right?"

Harmony stopped pulling at her bindings and glanced at the picture. She'd been looking at empty walls for so long that seeing a pop of color on all that white gave her a little rush of unexpected joy.

Lucky moved to bedside table. He opened the drawer and reached inside.

She tried to sit up. "Wait, what are you—"

"Bingo." Her vibrator. Baby blue. It looked so strange in Lucky's big hand that for a moment she wasn't sure it was hers. "And there's more," he said. "I like this brand." A bottle of lube, still sealed. She'd bought it on a whim right before her relationship hit the skids.

Lucky put both the lube and the vibrator on the bed next to her head, then returned to the drawer where he found a couple of condoms. "Nope. These won't work." He put them back and closed the drawer. "Stay here." He paused. "As if you had another option."

Harmony listened to his footsteps as he walked to the living room. In a moment, he reappeared at her side.

"See these?" He held a strip of Magnums in front of her face. "I bought these on my way here. How does that make you feel?"

Harmony looked at the golden wrappers. She didn't know what to say.

Lucky dropped the condoms next to her and stood up straight. He took his half-erect cock in his hand and stroked himself slowly. "Harmony." His voice had gone stern again. "How does that make you feel, knowing a man has come to you with ten condoms in his pocket, prepared to fuck you with all of them?"

She swallowed hard and stared at his dick. "It makes me feel..." She trailed off.

"Answer me."

"It makes me feel like a slut."

"You like that word, don't you?" He leaned down and kissed

her softly. "Is that what you want to be? Do you want to be a slut tonight?"

She gripped the belt in her cold hands and closed her eyes. Her pussy tingled, aching for his attention. "Yes."

He let go of his dick and climbed back on top of her. When his lips covered hers, Harmony melted, every muscle in her body gone slack. No one kissed like Lucky. With his lips and tongue, he ignited lightning in her brain, flashes in her memory of the complex layers of pleasure he knew how to build inside her. He kissed her neck and throat. With rough hands, he grabbed her breasts and kneaded them hard, teasing her nipples with his thumbs before he sucked on each of them, a minute apiece and back again.

By the time he got to her pussy, Harmony was pulled so tight she feared she would explode as soon as he touched her.

He seemed to read her mind. "Shh." His soft breath washed over her aching clit. Her nerve endings hummed as he spread her legs with his big hands. "Hold back for me, *belleza*."

"What if I can't?"

He looked up at her, hair disheveled, eyes bright with lust. "If you come too fast, you'll get a punishment. Understand?"

She met his gaze. Goose bumps covered her stomach and her nipples were erect. "I understand."

When his hot, wicked tongue glided up her slick seam, Harmony closed her eyes and arched her back. The headboard bucked when she yanked on it with her restraints. Lucky licked her clit, swiping his tongue back and forth, pausing only to suck on her pussy lips before returning to his task. His beard grew damp. Again and again, he brought her to the brink, but each time, she fought off the orgasm. She was sweating and panting, all of her concentration focused on holding back the tidal wave of her climax. She was soaked. Her entire body throbbed. When he sank a thick finger inside her, fireworks went off behind her eyelids. Her pussy fluttered, a breath away from coming. He withdrew his finger.

"Bad girl," he whispered. He sat up and leaned back on his knees. His cock stood straight up, ready for her. "Tell me, what are you?" His deep voice was hard again.

She was so turned on, she couldn't breathe. "A slut," she gasped.

In one smooth motion, he flipped her over onto her stomach. Roughly, he grabbed her hips and lifted her until she was on her knees. Her hands were still tied. She lay prostrate, worshipping the headboard, her ass high in the air. His hot body arched over her.

"Harmony," he whispered in her ear, "I've wanted to do this to you since we first played together." His rough palms slid down her back, thumbs slowly grazing her spine. He took each of her cheeks in his hands and squeezed hard enough to make her squirm. When he let go, the blood rushed back into them. "I'm going to spank you, *belleza.* Would you like that?"

Harmony closed her eyes in anticipation. She was trembling. "Yes."

He stroked her right cheek with his palm, lifted his hand, and brought it down with a loud smack. Harmony gasped. "I love that sound," he growled. He did again. When he switched and gave her left cheek two firm swats, Harmony groaned, confused by the powerful reaction of her body. Instead of pain, her brain registered arousal.

"You're wondering why you like it, right?" Lucky smacked her right cheek again, harder than before. "You're not supposed to, but you do. That's the great mystery. Why? There's no answer. Why does anything feel good? It just does." He bent down. Harmony could feel his breath against her hot, tingling skin. Gently, he kissed her right asscheek. "God, what a beautiful ass. Made for spanking."

The word came out before she realized she'd said it. "More."
She closed her eyes. "Give me more."

"Are you sure?"

"Please, Lucky."

He obliged her. With his work-hardened hands, he spanked
her until they were both panting and her tender skin was on fire.
Lucky gave her one more smack, reached down, and stroked her
dripping pussy. When he pressed two thick fingers into her, she
gasped. Pain and pleasure swirled together in her brain, each
sensation intensifying the other.

He leaned down, his chest hair grazing her back. As he thrust
his fingers inside her, he kissed the back of her neck and whispered, "Tell me something."

"What?"

He withdrew his fingers and ran the slick pads gently over her
asshole. "Ever had a man here?"

At the strange sensation, Harmony opened her eyes. "No."

"Would you like to?"

"I don't know." She blinked. "I've heard it hurts."

He kissed her neck again. "It can. But it can also feel good, if
you know what you're doing."

"Do you know what you're doing?" she whispered.

"I do." He massaged the delicate rim with his fingertips. She
gasped. "I'll make love to you here. Not tonight, but soon."

Not tonight, but soon. His words echoed in her ears as Lucky
grabbed a condom, tore it open, and sheathed himself. Desire,
hot and syrupy, filled her veins—this man. In her bed. Her lover,
and not just for tonight. The idea was almost too much to
process.

She arched her back as he took his place behind her. When the
tops of his thighs grazed the tender skin on her ass, she hissed. He
spanked her again and pain blazed up her spine, waking up every
nerve in her body. He took his cock in his hand and massaged her

pussy lips with its slick head. They groaned together. Then he put his hands on her waist, snapped his hips forward, and buried himself deep. Harmony gasped, speechless with sensation.

He rode her hard. The sound of their bodies smacking together filled the room. She felt herself straining, stretched to the limit around him. With each thrust, Harmony's soul loosened from her body, ready to fly.

He spanked her again and her pussy clenched hard around his shaft. Then she felt it—the cool drizzle of lube down her asscrack. Lucky tossed the bottle back on the mattress and spread the slippery liquid all over. He swirled her asshole with his thumb, then pressed the first joint inside her just as the head of his cock tapped her G-spot. Harmony's sense of control crumbled. A dozen more thrusts and she was a goner. A giant orgasm threatened to break inside her, blooming like a time-lapse rose.

"Lucky?" she gasped.

He speeded up his thrusts and pressed his thumb deeper. His accent was stronger now. "Yes. You can come now, *belleza.* Come all over me."

She exploded. She came so long and so absurdly hard that she and Lucky started to laugh, both of them too surprised to do anything else. There was no acting tough in this situation. As the orgasm ripped through her, he held her tight and kissed her neck. When the pleasure drained out of her at last, he withdrew from her body and untied her wrists. She collapsed onto him, blissful tears streaming down her face. She kissed his cheeks, his throat, and his chest. He grabbed her and kissed her lips. She was sweaty and gross but she didn't care—she didn't care about anything but him.

When the blood flowed back into her arms and her fingers stopped tingling, she slipped the condom off him and stroked him back to life. He leaned back with his hands behind his head, his handsome face smug with the knowledge that he'd just given her the biggest orgasm of her life.

When he was hard as steel in her fist, Harmony slid a fresh condom on him and gingerly climbed on top, fitting his cock into her tender pussy. She pivoted her hips gently and slid down. A muscle flexed in his jaw as he stared at her with those gorgeous, sleepy eyes. His chest rose and fell with each deep breath.

In the back of her mind, some ugly questions suddenly took shape. Did he always make love like this? Did he treat all of his lovers with this same blazing passion? Did he have a woman in every town, waiting for him the way she had waited for him, aching and hungry?

"Tell me something," she whispered.

"What?"

"Where did you learn to make love?"

"Here and there."

"On the road?" She put her hands on his rigid chest and began to ride him, gripping his shaft as tightly as she could.

"Yes." He groaned.

"You must've been with lots of women."

"Why? Do you like how I fuck you?" He reached behind her, grabbed her vibrator and turned it on. The quiet, familiar hum of her toy made her body clench automatically. He rested one hand on her hip. With the other hand, he held the tip of her vibrator gently against her clit. A fresh rush of arousal slid out of her pussy down his shaft. "Those other women? Practice."

"For what?"

"For you, you beautiful slut." He pressed her clit harder. "Ride me and make yourself come again."

She rode him like she was running from the devil. Abs flexed, she canted her hips back and forth, slapping her inner thighs against his hips. She leaned back and rested her hands on his knees, giving him better access to her clit. When he began to draw circles on her with the toy, she seized up yet again. Her whole body ached, stretched tight around him, balanced precariously on the edge of another big climax.

Suddenly, he sat up and flipped her onto her back. She looked up at him breathlessly. Giving each of her nipples a wet, greedy suckle, he lifted himself on one massive arm and began to pound her like jackhammer.

"Hold it," he growled. "Hold your toy."

She grabbed the slippery vibrator and held it in place, eyes wide. Lucky slid his hands under her ass and lifted her off the mattress. He leaned forward, bending her into a C. He put all of his weight on her and began to fuck her harder than she'd ever been fucked before.

She came in seconds. Every muscle flexed, Lucky came with her, sweating and swearing, thrusting like an animal. The friction of his big cock inside her prolonged her orgasm, drawing it out into eternity. The contractions of her climax were so powerful, she feared Lucky had tied knots inside her that would never be undone.

When they were finished, Lucky took her vibrator from her hand and withdrew slowly from her body. He got up from the bed and walked to her bathroom. She listened as he turned on the shower and returned to the bedroom.

He leaned down and kissed her lips. "Come with me."

She took his hand and followed him down her own hallway. They climbed into the shower together. She hissed when the warm water hit her tender skin. She almost lost her footing on the tiles and he caught her.

"Be careful," he whispered, smiling. "Lube is slippery."

Lucky held her against his chest and kissed her forehead as water rained down on them. She wrapped her arms around his waist and leaned against him. He was so solid, so strong—rooted to the earth, as if nothing could ever knock him over. They washed each other in silence, celebrating each caress with another sweet kiss. Lucky turned off the taps and toweled her off. She was drowsy, high on sex. She kissed his lips and he lifted her once more into his arms.

Then she was in her own bed, under the covers, snuggled up against his warm, beautiful body.

"Lucky?"

"Sí, belleza."

"What time are you leaving tomorrow?" She closed her eyes.

"Early. Four."

"Don't leave without saying goodbye."

"I won't." He yawned and stroked her cheek. "Sleep now, Harmony. Sweet dreams."

-⚘-

THEY WOKE up together in the dark.

Lucky slid between her legs again, feasting on her. His hot tongue circled her clit, then slid deep into her pussy, curling inside her, licking her awake.

She tried to sit up. His big hands pushed her gently back down into the pillows. Then his fingertips found her nipples. He circled her areolas and pinched the tips gently as he suckled her clit. She was so wet, her inner thighs grew slick against his cheeks.

A deep moan vibrated in her throat. She stopped fighting and lay back as he played with her, putting his fingers and tongue wherever he wanted, drawing pleasure out of her body wherever he touched her.

She listened as he tore open another condom and slid it on. When he fed his cock into her, she gasped, still incredulous how something so big and long could fit inside her, much less feel so good.

They didn't talk. He leaned over her, pinning her hips to the mattress. When he kissed her, she tasted her own sweet pussy on his tongue. The flavor aroused her. She could hear herself straining wetly around him as he made slow, shallow thrusts into her body. She embraced him, running her palms over his broad, muscular back and squeezing his rock-hard ass. He hypnotized her with his kisses. When he changed his angle and deepened his thrusts, she came without warning, a soul-wrenching climax that seized her from the tips of her toes to the top of her head. Hot pleasure flooded her bloodstream. Still kissing her, he froze and came just seconds later, gasping for air against her lips. She ran her hands through his hair and kissed his cheeks, his chin, and his jaw.

When his climax receded at last, he lifted his head and pulled out slowly. Her body ached as he withdrew. After he went to the bathroom to clean up, he turned off the light and lay back down behind her, spooning her close. He kissed her shoulder. "I want to see you when I get back."

"When?"

"Five days." Another kiss. "Five long days."

Her heart began to beat faster. She'd always been good at keeping her cards close to her chest when it came to feelings. Tonight, did she have the courage to say what she really felt? "Lucky?"

"*Sí, belleza.*"

Should she tell him what she'd been thinking? How would he react? "I have to tell you something."

"Hmm."

She turned around to face him. The words came slowly. "I don't know where you are in your life right now. I don't know what you're looking for." His forehead was cool to the touch as she combed back his messy hair with her fingers. "But I don't want you to think that we're just a rebound. Or that I'm using you, like I did the first night we were together."

"I know." He took her hand and kissed it. "Do you believe me when I say I like you?"

She was glad it was dark so he didn't have to see her blush. "Yes," she said quietly. "I believe you."

"And how about you? Do you like me?"

Harmony lay motionless as she considered his question. Her heart was still sore over her breakup. Had she truly recovered from Frank? Was she starting something new with Lucky with a clear mind and a clear heart? Or was she too mixed up to make a real decision? She didn't want to start a new relationship if it was going to be poisoned by the one that came before. Lucky was a good man. He didn't deserve to be treated unfairly.

Before she could say anything, Lucky squeezed her hand. "You know what? Don't answer that. I'm sorry."

"No, it's not that—"

He kissed her forehead. "Listen. I have to go or I won't make it on time." He let go of her hand and slipped out of bed.

"Lucky, wait—"

"*Belleza*, don't worry about it. There will be plenty of time to talk when I get back. There's no rush." His voice was soft, as comforting as the warm covers he tucked around her body. He was quiet for a moment as he looked down at her. "I'll miss you."

Her heart had taken a beating in the last few days. Now it ached like a wound opened up before it could heal. "I'll miss you too." She wished she could tell him everything she was feeling. She longed to start fresh and give him the attention he deserved, but now wasn't the time. "Good luck."

Wide awake in the dark, she listened as he got dressed in the living room. He turned off the lights in the hallway, opened her front door, and closed it with a soft click. She heard his truck start on the silent street below. Harmony couldn't understand the overwhelming sadness that hit her when the rumble of his engine faded away.

ON HER DAY OFF, Harmony woke up early. After a pit stop at Starbucks, she visited the local supermarket and bought three bunches of flowers—pink carnations, red dahlias, and golden sunflowers. She climbed into her Jeep and drove to Oleander as the sun rose over the hills.

Cece MacKinnon sat on the front step of the farmhouse, a bouquet of wildflowers lying across her knees. She wore a sundress and sandals. Her long brown hair was loose. Sunlight illuminated the gray streaks in it. When Harmony approached, she hopped up and climbed into the Jeep with the energy of a woman much younger than fifty-five.

"Good morning, Auntie Cece." Harmony kissed Cece's cheek. "Ready to go?"

"I'm ready."

Oleander Cemetery was a short drive away. They arrived just as the groundskeeper unlocked the gates. Harmony parked in the small lot by the mausoleum and together, she and Cece took the familiar path to the northwest corner, their arms full of flowers.

As they walked, Cece talked softly about the work the boys were doing on the ranch and the public outreach Georgia was doing to build the MacKinnon Ranch brand. Laughing, she told a funny story about her grandson Derek, who'd developed a crush on a little girl in his first grade class.

"Starting early?" Harmony said.

"A little late, actually. These MacKinnon boys—always crushing on somebody. Every last one of them."

"Starting with Uncle Dale?" said Harmony with a gentle smile. "Well, crushing on one girl, anyway."

Cece threaded her arm through Harmony's. "Yes. Starting with my Dale."

The three graves were close to each other. Together, Cece and Harmony removed the old flowers and brushed away the dust and leaves on the headstones. Harmony laid out the flowers she'd brought. Pink carnations for her mother, who loved the color pink. Red dahlias for her father, who'd planted dahlias in their yard when she was a child. And sunflowers for Dale—the flower seemed just right for his sunny personality and shaggy head of blond hair.

The ground was still damp with dew, so Harmony stood in between her parents' gravestones. Her father had died when she was very young, but her mother had passed away only two years ago, very suddenly, from pneumonia. They'd been close. Harmony missed her every day, but coming to the cemetery didn't make her sad—other things did. Seeing mothers and daughters, out and about together. A beautiful pair of shoes in a store window. Garth Brooks or Clint Black on the country radio station—her mother's favorite singers.

Cece put the bouquet of wildflowers in the vase on Dale's gravestone. She knelt down on the wet grass, placed her hand on the stone, and began to talk quietly. To give her privacy, Harmony took a walk through the silent cemetery. The newer section was made up of flat grave markers, but the older section was made up of big cement headstones worn away by the desert wind—Oleander's first residents, its founders and the Dust Bowl migrants who'd built it up. So many names, so many stories.

When Harmony returned, Cece was wiping away her tears with a handkerchief she'd brought in her purse. Harmony's heart ached for her. Cece and Dale had been perfectly matched, lion tamer and lion. She couldn't imagine the grief Cece felt when he'd passed away.

Cece got to her feet and Harmony gave her a hug. Together they walked slowly back to the Jeep.

"What do you miss the most about Uncle Dale?" Harmony asked quietly.

"Some of my friends at church asked me that the other day," Cece said. "The obvious answer is the physical aspect of our relationship. He was a demon in the sack."

Harmony put her hand across her chest in mock shock. "Auntie Cece! I never."

"Silly girl." Cece smacked her playfully with the back of her hand and sniffed. "Dale and I—we had always been affectionate. I miss that. I think I always will." A mockingbird flew down from a eucalyptus tree and drank from a puddle near the walkway. Cece continued, "I miss him at unexpected moments. Like when I drink my coffee in the morning, I miss preparing his Thermos—he drank his coffee without cream, but with four spoonfuls of sugar. Four spoonfuls! No wonder he was always so hyper." She smiled to herself. "I miss watching him cleaning his rifle after a hunting trip. He was always so careful about it. He'd lay out all of his equipment, sit down, and take his time. He'd listen to the Dodgers on the radio. Sometimes the boys would watch him. He was so patient with them." She tightened her grip on Harmony's arm. "Most of all, I miss him very early in the morning. That's when we'd talk. Quietly. Under the covers. Before the boys were up. Before all the chaos of the day. Our little pocket of peace. Just me and him."

A tear rolled down Harmony's cheek. Cece noticed it. "Now you cut that out." She gave Harmony's arm a gentle squeeze. "If you don't, I'll start up again and we'll drown each other in tears."

They continued down the pathway in silence as Harmony thought about what Cece had said. Again, she gathered up her courage. "Auntie Cece," she said at last. "I need your advice."

"What's the matter?"

Harmony took a deep breath and told her about Lucky, starting with the night she broke up with Dr. Dreamboat and ending with Lucky leaving her apartment for Arizona. She left out the more lurid details, but Auntie Cece was sharp—she'd have no problem connecting the dots.

By the time Harmony finished, they were standing by the Jeep. Cece said nothing for a little while, nodding to herself as she contemplated the story. The sun had risen high over the horizon and the air was beginning to warm up. "So what is it exactly that you're afraid of?" she asked Harmony at last.

"I'm afraid to start something new with Lucky. I was with

Frank for a year. Am I just running from one man to another because I'm afraid to be alone?" Harmony paused. She thought of the fierce and quiet devotion Lucky had for his family, the gentle regard he had for his horse. For all his swagger, he was the real deal—a breath of fresh air. "I'm worried that whatever I start with Lucky will be poisoned by the relationship I had with Frank. What if I don't heal properly because I didn't give myself enough time?"

"What would be enough time?"

Feeling lame, Harmony referred to an article she'd read on the Internet. "Between relationships, I've heard you should wait a month for every year you were with your ex."

Cece looked at her with skepticism. "'A month for every year,'" she repeated. "Says who?"

Harmony gave her a sheepish shrug. "People."

"People, huh? Tell me. The way you feel about Lucky, do you think this is just a fling?"

She shook her head. "No. I don't."

"And how about Lucky? Is he interested in starting something serious with you?"

"I think so, but I can't be sure." She sighed. She wished she could look into men's brains and see what they were thinking. It would make life infinitely easier for everyone. "But I used him, Auntie Cece." Guilt washed over Harmony yet again. "I used him to make myself feel better. Like he was an object, not even a person."

"It's good you're acknowledging that. But knowing Lucky, I'm guessing he didn't mind being used by you," said Cece. "That boy's carried a torch for you for years."

Years—Harmony'd had no idea. Even her Auntie Cece had known how Lucky felt. "But that's bad karma, though, isn't it? Turning a rebound into a relationship? Shouldn't I give it more time?"

"There's never a good time for anything, Harmony." Cece

leaned against the Jeep and smoothed down her dress. "Hey, want to know a secret?"

"What?"

"Now this is something no one knows but me, Dale, and Dr. Lamont." Cece smiled. "You ready?"

Harmony nodded, her interest piqued. "Sure."

"Dean—he wasn't born premature. He was born right on time."

"You mean you were—?"

Cece nodded. "Big church wedding. Behind that bouquet I was three months pregnant. Dean was the reason Dale and I got married. Neither of us had planned on any of it. To tell the truth, neither of us was particularly keen on getting hitched. We had no idea if it was the right decision. We did it anyway. And looking at how our lives turned out, it was the best decision we could've made." She wagged a finger at Harmony. "Don't you go spreading that news around, Harmony Santos. It might have been thirty-eight years ago, but Oleander loves its scandals wherever it can get them."

"I won't say a word," said Harmony.

"Now you listen to me. You say that you used Lucky. But there's another side of that equation. Lucky gave himself to you that night." She paused. "I'm going to say a word that scares young people. Are you ready?"

Harmony nodded.

"That's what love is, dear. Giving. Back and forth. You give and he gives, replenishing each other. Making each other stronger, every day. Do you understand?" She took Harmony's hand. "I never knew the joy of daughters until you and Melody came into my life. Your sister's crazy and you're even crazier, but even if you were my own blood, I couldn't love you more. Here's the advice I have to give you. Look where we're standing." She motioned to the gravestones around them. "Life is short. Like I said, there's never a good time for anything. So don't you ever be afraid to give. Don't you ever be afraid to say what's in your heart. And most of all—listen to me, Harmony Santos—don't you ever be afraid to love."

—◦—

PAYSON. Round ten. The deepening sky threatened another psychedelic Arizona sunset. The rodeo arena was full. Excitement infused the pine-scented air. After checking his rigging for the hundredth time, Lucky sat still in his saddle and tried to relax behind the bustling chutes.

Breathe. Stay sharp.

This was a big show, one of the oldest in the country. Tonight, Lucky and his closest competitor, a two-time world finals qualifier from Oklahoma named Tanner Thomas, were duking it out for a spot at this year's world finals. Round for round, they chased each other in the standings, coming up neck-and-neck at last, adding drama to the highly technical tie-down roping event. This was their last chance to accumulate the winnings that would determine whether they made it to world finals or stayed home and watched the other guy on TV.

But for Lucky, this final round meant much more than a trip to Vegas and a gold buckle. He'd never come this close to finals in all the years he'd been a calf roper. This was a chance to prove to himself that he'd made it—that he belonged here just as much as the next cowboy.

His horse nickered. He rubbed Batman's neck and looked once again at the standings. The time to beat was 8.2 seconds. Three more ropers were up before him. He was second-to-last. Tanner had the last spot this go-round.

Moments like this Lucky relied on the discipline he'd built up over years of competition. Long hours on the road, variations in weather and other environmental conditions, equipment failure, bad horse days—lots of things conspired to ruin a performance.

The one constant was a cowboy's attitude. And he'd worked hard to earn full control over his.

Well...except for one thing. He reached into his pocket and checked his phone. No calls.

Ever since he'd arrived in Arizona, Lucky texted Harmony every night. He liked to send her photos. Batman smiling, oats in her teeth. Sunset over the pines. The one lunchtime he splurged on a piece of fry bread. In response, Harmony sent him photos too. A colorful thank-you card drawn by a little girl who'd had an appendectomy. A pair of fancy pink cowboy boots in a store window. A pancake she'd made for herself that looked inadvertently like Mike Wazowski. And once—Lucky would never delete the photo, as long as he lived—a morning selfie in her silk robe, raising a glass of orange juice to toast his performance.

She called him twice—late-night phone calls, her voice sweet and sexy in his ear. As they talked about their days and teased each other, he lay on the lumpy mattress in his trailer, looking out his tiny window at stars twinkling in the dark blue sky. He was pretty damn sure he was falling in love.

Yesterday, he'd gone on a walk to clear his head. On a well-kept residential street in Payson, he'd found a small patch of purple flowers growing in the front yard of a house. He'd snapped a quick photo and texted it to Harmony. *Just like your painting, right? Thinking of you.*

Then...nothing. She hadn't called or texted back since. This was his big night. He'd checked his phone more times than he cared to admit. A small part of him was annoyed, both at himself and at her. But why? They weren't together. She had no obligation to keep playing with him. And she was busy—her hours at the hospital were tough.

Lucky tucked his phone away and frowned at himself. *Get your head in the game.*

For all his experience, he'd never had a girlfriend. An unpredictable future and distinct lack of resources had long kept him from pursuing anything serious. Which seemed fine by the women he'd known—they were content to fade in and out of his life, interested only in what he could offer them in bed.

But Harmony. She was different. She'd always been different.

He'd call her tonight after the final round. Whatever the results, this rodeo had already lodged itself in his memory as one of his favorites—the first time he'd come close to qualifying for world finals, but also the first time he hadn't felt lonely on the road, all because of the girl on the other side of his phone. Whatever lay in the future for them, he'd always have this time to remember. For now, that was enough.

Another roper completed his run. Some trouble flanking the calf had resulted in a 12.3 time. Batman nickered again, as if she understood that there was one fewer person standing between them and finals.

"Garcia!"

Lucky turned around. By the chutes stood a team roper whose name Lucky couldn't remember. "What's up?"

"Someone's looking for you." The man pointed behind Lucky at the stands.

Confused, Lucky turned around and squinted into the slanting sunlight. He lowered the brim of his hat to get a better look at the faces in the crowd. Leaning way over the rails were three women, waving and whistling at him.

One of the other calf ropers laughed at him. "Some of your groupies, Luck?"

Lucky walked Batman over. Closer to the stands, the women came into focus.

No way.

His mother. His sister. And standing between them, Harmony, an enormous smile on her face.

Joy and surprise surged inside him. Barriers separated them, but he would've jumped over anything to reach them if he could. "What are you guys doing here?"

"We wanted to surprise you!" Araceli shouted. "We almost didn't make it, but Harmony drives like a maniac!"

He looked from Harmony to his sister to his mother. "Where are you sitting?"

"Over there!" His sister pointed out a section in the bleachers.

Applause filled the arena. Another roper had just finished his run—and a good one too. Now the new time to beat was 7.9 seconds. Lucky's heart ached, pulled in too many directions. "I'm almost up." He was at a loss for words. "I'll find you afterwards."

"Good luck!" shouted Harmony. A golden slash of sunshine fell across her beautiful face as she turned one last time to wave at him. "We'll be cheering for you!"

Lucky watched as they disappeared back into the crowd. Then he turned his attention back to the calf-roping box. The roper before him was about to start his run. Still giddy with surprise, Lucky made his way over to the box.

A few seconds later and the next roper was done too. His horse dragged the calf too far. The best time for the round was still 7.9 seconds. And now it was Lucky's turn.

As he got into the rider's box, Lucky adjusted his feet in his stirrups and got his ropes in order. Standing against the back wall, Batman was still, her eyes on the breakaway nylon barrier stretched across the open side of the box. A handler stood in the box with Lucky, all three of them waiting as the calf was placed in its adjacent chute.

Ten thousand hours of practice. Muscle memory. Discipline. Desire. All of it came together in this moment. Lucky clenched the piggin' string in his teeth. Heart booming in his chest, he gave his nod.

The calf bolted out. Lucky swung his lasso. The barrier was released, and Batman exploded out of the box, all of her attention focused on the little black calf.

Lucky roped the calf, closed the loop, and pitched his slack. The calf stayed on its feet, facing the horse. Lucky dismounted off the right side of Batman and raced down the rope anchored to his saddle. As Batman kept the rope taut, Lucky flanked the calf and grabbed three of its legs as it fought him. Time seemed to slow down. Lucky rallied. After two lightning-fast wraps and a hooey, he threw his hands in the air to stop the clock. He remounted Batman and put slack in the rope. The calf kicked but couldn't get free.

The crowd erupted. His time appeared on the scoreboard.

Adrenaline still pounding in his bloodstream, Lucky looked up at last.

Holy shit.

He'd performed a textbook run. And he'd done it fast—7.1 seconds. One of his best times all season.

Lucky took off his hat and waved at the crowd as their cheers roared in his ears. He faced the section where his family sat and blew kisses towards them, even though he couldn't spot them from where he stood. He exited the arena and exhaled at last.

Now for the last run. Tanner Thomas. The rangy Oklahoman was in his mid-thirties. Years of experience showed in his technique. On the circuit, Lucky and Tanner had become good friends. Calf-roping was an event built on technical ability. But when rankings depended on tenths of a second, luck affected results just as much as skill.

Lucky rubbed Batman's neck once more. "Good girl," he whispered. "Let's see what happens now."

LUCKY'S PERFORMANCE took Harmony's breath away. Tall and handsome in the saddle, he wore a black cowboy hat, jeans, boots, and a long-sleeve shirt decorated with patches from his sponsors. He clenched a rope in his teeth. When the calf broke free, he swung his lasso and roped it in a heartbeat. She gasped when he did a flying dismount and sprinted towards the calf.

Muscles bulging, he picked up and threw the 250-pound calf. He had tied its legs so fast, she didn't even see him do it.

When his run was finished, Araceli and Harmony jumped up cheering. They hugged each other when his time appeared on the scoreboard. And they screamed like maniacs when the announcers said he'd taken over the first-place spot for Round 10. Lucky's mother grabbed Harmony's hand and gave it a squeeze. Her eyes were bright with happiness.

This trip had been one of the wildest things Harmony had ever done. At exactly four o'clock yesterday afternoon, she was leaving the hospital, bone tired after another long shift. Her phone buzzed. She took it out and looked at the text.

Just like your painting, right? Thinking of you.

Was it possible to fall in love with someone over a text? Harmony wasn't a romantic. Never had been. But the snapshot Lucky sent had stopped her in her tracks. Bright purple flowers, sage green leaves. The picture was so beautiful, her heart leaped.

The same old arguments bubbled up in her head. Common knowledge stated that rebounds weren't meant to last. She and Frank had been together for a year. Wasn't she supposed to spend time on her own to regroup and get right with the world? Wasn't she supposed to need space from men? By that school of thought, any relationship she started with Lucky would be doomed from the start.

But no one had ever made her feel this way before.

The sex was spectacular—no doubt about that. And these few days spent apart from him had given her time to think about Lucky in a different context. His texts made her smile. She looked forward to their nighttime conversations—he was funny and observant, as smart as he was sexy. Frank was smart, but Lucky was smart in a different way. Instead of using his intelligence to separate himself from the world the way Frank did, Lucky used his intelligence to become more connected to the people around him. His heart was wide open.

Auntie Cece's words echoed in her ears. *Life is short. There's never a good time for anything. So don't you ever be afraid to give. Don't you ever be afraid to love.*

In that moment, Harmony knew the truth. Lucky had given himself to her their first night together. Now it was her turn—she could give something back to him.

She got on the phone. First, she called her boss and requested some last-minute time off. She called Araceli and her mother to make impromptu arrangements for Arizona. She called Georgia and asked to borrow the MacKinnons' minivan. In a frantic rush, she took the minivan for an oil change, gassed it up, washed it, and vacuumed out the Cheerios. She looked up Payson on her GPS and made a room reservation at the local Indian casino and resort.

Wired on caffeine and her own recklessness, Harmony picked up Lucky's mother and sister in the morning and drove eight hours straight to see her man. And even though this was crazy and impulsive—crazy and impulsive even for her—she'd known in her heart it was the right thing to do.

The announcer introduced the final rider. Tanner Thomas from Oklahoma.

In the stands, Araceli grabbed Harmony's other hand. The three women, linked together by Lucky, stared expectantly at the last rider in the box.

His white hat bobbed as the rider nodded. The calf broke free and the horse lunged after it.

As soon as it had started, it was over. Tanner Thomas had tied the calf. When his time went up, Harmony's heart tumbled out of her chest.

Seven seconds flat. The two-time world finals qualifier had qualified for Las Vegas yet again. The stands thundered with applause.

"One tenth of a second?" Araceli got to her feet, an indignant scowl on her face. "What the heck?"

Lucky's mother took Araceli's hand and said something to her in Spanish.

"But it's not fair, *Mamá!*" the teenager said. Tears welled in her eyes. "He worked so hard for this. Harder than anyone."

Her mother nodded and embraced her. Araceli sobbed and wiped her eyes with the Kleenex that had appeared magically out of her mother's purse.

"Come on," Harmony said softly. "Let's go see Lucky."

SECOND PLACE CAME with a check for three grand—much-needed money for Araceli's college fund. Happy not to come up empty-handed, Lucky treated Harmony, his mother, and his sister to a hamburger dinner in town. As he drove them back to the hotel, he laughed at the bug-spattered windshield of the minivan, the chocolate bar wrappers and empty boxes of coconut water stashed under the seats, and the Taylor Swift and Carrie Underwood playing on loop through the speakers.

"I still can't believe you're all here," he said in both English and Spanish.

He took advantage of their hotel room and enjoyed a much-needed hot shower. Then the girls got ready and he brought them all to the rodeo dance. Live music, soda, beer, and cowboys —Araceli squealed and ran straight to the dance floor, their mother keeping an eagle eye on his precocious and pretty seventeen-year-old sister.

After a lazy two-step, Lucky lowered his lips to Harmony's ear. "Want to take a walk with me?"

She looked into his eyes and nodded.

They walked hand-in-hand past the parking lot and the edge of the rodeo grounds. The fresh mountain air was cold and Lucky hung his jacket on Harmony's shoulders. Their boots crunched on the pitted asphalt. The night sky was clear, studded with bright, fat stars.

When they were out among the shadowy pines, Lucky leaned against a tree, pulled Harmony close, and kissed her long and deep. He stroked her cold cheeks and the warm skin on the back of her neck underneath her hair. She wrapped her arms around him and sighed, a soft, sweet sound that pierced his heart. This girl had driven almost six hundred miles to see him. She'd even thought to bring his mother and his sister to watch him compete —a luxury for a family that needed to save every penny.

Seeing Harmony and Araceli laughing together at dinner made funny things happen in his chest. *Happiness* was not an adequate word for what he felt in this moment. *Complete* came close. And there was a third word he could use—but maybe it was too soon to bring that word up.

He broke their kiss and embraced her tightly, resting his chin on her head as he stroked her back.

"Thank you," he said. "Thank you so much."

They held each other for a long time, the silence of the forest descending over them. "You're amazing," she said at last. "I can't believe you can do all that."

"It's just practice."

"How'd you tie that calf so fast?"

"It's not hard. Two wraps and a hooey." He smiled. "I'll show you later."

She sniffed, a little puff of breath against his throat. "We have to find a way for you to keep Batman. You can't give this up. I was thinking about Araceli the other day. I'm still in touch with the recruiters at my nursing school. I emailed one of them and she's going to send me some applications for scholarships. If Araceli gets an internship at the hospital this summer, her supervisors can recommend her for the scholarship. I can too."

As he held her, Lucky could feel Harmony's heart beating faster. She was excited about helping his sister.

He loved his family more than anything in the world. But looking after them had been a difficult, often lonely job. To have someone on his side at last—warmth flooded his chest. This woman was amazing.

"I need to tell you something," he said.

"What?"

"I'm not giving up rodeo. I'm not selling Batman."

She pulled away from him. Her eyes were luminous in the moonlight. "You're not?"

"No, *belleza*. I was going to tell you this in person when I got home."

"Tell me what?"

"I talked to Dean MacKinnon three days ago. He needs someone to take over the horse-training program at Walker-MacKinnon Ranch. We've worked together for years, so he hired me for the position. It's a full-time job. Benefits, retirement, boarding for Batman, flexibility to compete in rodeos, even a place to live on the property in Lake Isabella. And more money in one year than I've ever made in all my jobs put together." He paused. "Araceli can go to nursing school now. No doubt about it."

Harmony jumped up into his arms and squealed with laughter. He struggled to keep his hold on her as she covered his face with kisses. "I can't believe you waited to tell me that! I was so heartbroken when I saw Tanner Thomas's time posted. Your sister was crying. Have you told them yet?"

"No, not yet."

"Lucky!"

"I'll tell them tomorrow."

"That's just cruel."

"A little bit. They'll be okay." He smiled. "But right now, I need to tell you something else."

She froze. "What now?"

Gently, he set her back down on her feet and kissed her forehead. "It's kind of big. Are you ready?"

"Yes. I'm ready." She took a deep breath.

"I have to whisper it. That's how big it is." He bent down and brushed his lips against her tiny earlobe. "I want you to be my girlfriend. What do you think?"

To Lucky's surprise, Harmony didn't answer him. She grabbed the front of his shirt and kissed him so slowly and thoroughly that he lost himself in her, adrift on a fever dream. She didn't answer him as they walked back to the rodeo grounds in the dark. She didn't answer him as he undressed her in his trailer, or as he made love to her like the universe was collapsing around them, her moans echoing in his ears as she came again and again and again.

Hours later, they lay on the bed in his trailer, tangled in each other. They were looking through the little window at the same stars he'd stared at when they talked over the phone.

"Yes," she whispered at last. "I want to be your girlfriend. Very much."

Lucky lay still as Harmony slowly fell asleep in his arms. His thoughts moved from one image to another. His father walking out the door for the last time. The plum tree in the backyard, heavy with fruit. His siblings howling in the dark as he struggled to put new batteries in the flashlight.

Now new images faded into the old ones. Cattle in a dew-covered pasture. His horse's golden-red coat, twitching as he brushed it. Harmony in her purple dress, laughing at some asinine thing he'd said. His mother crying as Abel translated his university acceptance letter to her. His brother and sister giggling in the dark as he made funny faces in the single beam of the flashlight.

Harmony snuggled against his chest and sighed softly.

He stared up at the stars. Destiny. Fortune. Karma. He didn't believe in any of it. But he did believe in love. And he knew no one loved like he did. When the time was right, he'd tell this girl the truth—he knew she was brave enough to face love head-on, just like he did.

"Good night, Lucky," she murmured.

Love filled his body, infusing his bloodstream with pure light. "Good night, *belleza*."

Continue reading for a preview of
Cowboy Player

EXCERPT FROM COWBOY PLAYER

"I'm immune to your charms, MacKinnon."

"That so?"

Her cheeks were warm. From the flirting or the gin? "Yup," she said, meeting his gaze. "Like a little clownfish in the gooey tentacles of a sea anemone."

"Really? Let's test that theory out." He put his glass down on the coffee table, wiped his hands on his jeans, and climbed on top of her. Straddling her legs with his thick thighs, he put on a duck face and began to do a goofy lap dance, gyrating his hips like a stripper.

She couldn't help it. She began to laugh. "Oh my God. Cut it out, you weirdo."

He put both hands behind his head and began to undulate his torso. "Feeling tingly yet? Has paralysis set in?"

Giggling, she tried to push him away without spilling her drink. "No, but you're giving me the heebie-jeebies."

"I fuckin' love it when you talk like my nana, Mel. It's so sexy in a deeply twisted, Freudian way." He began to hump her knee. "Tell me you're wearing granny panties. Whisper it in my ear."

She put her hand on his chest and tried to wiggle away,

laughing too hard to be turned on. "I can't imagine how other women resist you."

"Me neither. It's never happened before." Grinning, he put his big hands on her shoulders and kissed her cheek. On the record player, the next track started. Guitar licks, drums, a little fiddle— Melody knew the song at once.

"Oh man," said Clark. "'Troubadour'. This a good one. Dance with me, Mel."

He pulled her off the sofa before she could say anything. Wrapped up in the arms of a big cowboy was not a terrible place to be, so Melody danced with him, barefoot in her parents' living room, the slow two-step a song both their bodies knew the words to. Her laughter died away, giving way to a quiet sense of vulnerability. The verses slid by like a dream, erasing the burden of loneliness she'd been carrying for so long. It had been months since she'd been this close to a man. It had been years since she'd *felt* this close to one.

Clark could read her mind. "So what was his name again?" he asked softly. "Scott?"

"Yeah."

"What happened?"

"A slow-motion disaster, that's what happened." She rested her cheek against the hard, hot wall of Clark's chest. "He was a musician. Fun. Exciting. He said I meant the world to him. But I suppose the world wasn't enough."

"What do you mean?"

It was still hard to say aloud. "He cheated on me. It had been going on for months. When I found out and confronted him about it, he broke down said he was sorry. We tried to put it past us. We even went to therapy. But it was all a lie. He left me when my mom passed away." At first, the pain had been excruciating, dulled only by grief and the weight of her new responsibilities. "Eight years, down the drain."

"That's a long time. Did you ever talk about getting married?"

"He said he didn't like labels." She sighed. "Which was also a lie, because he married the other woman in Vegas in February."

"Jesus Christ. I'm sorry." Clark gave her a squeeze. "You know, if you were mine, I'd hold on to you for good."

"Sure. Until the next piece of ass came along."

"Never seen a piece of ass like yours."

"That's the friend talking. Your dick might say otherwise."

"My dick, huh?" Clark laughed quietly. "You're welcome to check with my dick yourself. He doesn't talk loud, so you'll have to get down on your knees to hear him."

"Jackass."

"Seriously, Mel. You don't know what you've got going on. Smart as all get-out. Hell, you run circles around me, and I'm a genius. And you're funny too. You make me laugh all the time."

She rolled her eyes. "Aw shucks, Ma. Next the cowboy told me I was real purty."

"Fuck pretty. You're beautiful."

It was too much. *Danger.* "Clark—"

"So beautiful. I always thought so." He gave her a sad smile. "Honest to God."

The heat rising between them cooked her brain. She was at a loss for words. "Thanks."

"No thanks needed. Just stating the obvious." They danced until the song ended on a ribbon of steel guitar. Clark leaned down and pressed his lips to her temple.

Melody gasped.

Instead of pulling away, he traced a slow, agonizing trail of kisses along her hairline until he was kissing her neck just behind her ear.

Pleasure overloaded her nervous system, but her brain wouldn't let her enjoy it. "Wh-what are you doing?"

"Something I've wanted to do for a long, long time."

"Oh God." She gripped his rigid arms. Complicated feelings

cascaded through her so quickly, she couldn't identify one from the other.

Still holding her, he looked into her eyes. "Don't be scared," he whispered. "Look at me."

For the first time in twenty-eight years, she realized Clark's eyes were brown. No—not brown. Swirled mahogany and gold, like bird's-eye maple, with irises rimmed in dark chocolate. Her body ached under his warm gaze, ravenous for what he offered her but terrified of what they'd lose if she took it.

"We're friends," she said. "I don't want to throw that away."

"Nothing will change that." He searched her face. "Do you think I'd hurt you?"

"Not intentionally." Loneliness welled up inside her. Her heart was a broken bucket at the bottom of a deep well. "And I know what it's like when you think you know someone, and then you discover…" She trailed off.

"But you know me," he said. "I'm not hiding anything. You know me better than anyone, right?"

She nodded.

He was quiet for a moment. "One night's not forever, Mel." The expression on his face was unreadable. "We're adults."

"Yeah, but—"

"If you don't want this, tell me no and I will back off."

She closed her eyes. Could she? Should she? Lust flooded her bloodstream. "What if…I don't want to tell you no?" she whispered.

He pressed his body against hers. At once she felt his desire for her, hard and real and burning against her belly.

"Then tell me yes," he murmured.

Desire trumped fear. She wanted this. She wanted him. Melody took a deep breath and opened her eyes. "Yes."

ABOUT THE AUTHOR

Mia Hopkins writes lush romances starring fun, sexy characters who love to get down and dirty. Her award-winning books have been featured by many publications including *The Washington Post*, *USA Today* and *Entertainment Weekly*. She lives in Los Angeles with her family.

For more information...
www.miahopkinsauthor.com

@miahopkinsxoxo